Fern wondered what it would be like to have a beautiful, button-nosed babe of her own.

The miracle of human birth was an unknown. Fern knew enough to understand that it began with a woman…and a man.

She could see only one side of Paul's face as he gazed down at his daughter. What would it be like to have a child with this oh-so-handsome man? No sooner had the thought entered her head that Fern was besieged with a forceful sensation.

Oh, my! Her thoughts were imposing a transformation. She was going to become human. Right now!

Panic had her winging toward the doorway. She barely got to safety when she changed into flesh and blood.

"Be still my heart," she whispered.

All this time she'd thought that it had been because of the baby that she had the ability to turn human. But it wasn't wee Katy at all.

"It's been Paul all along."

D0451021

Dear Reader,

Are you headed to the beach this summer? Don't forget to take along your sunblock—and this month's four new heartwarming love stories from Silhouette Romance!

Make Myrna Mackenzie's *The Black Knight's Bride* (SR #1722) the first book in your tote bag. This is the third story in THE BRIDES OF RED ROSE, a miniseries in which classic legends are retold in the voices of today's heroes and heroines. For a single mom fleeing her ex-husband, Red Rose seems like the perfect town—no men! But then she meets a brooding ex-soldier with a heart of gold....

In *Because of Baby* (SR #1723), a pixie becomes so enamored with a single dad and his adorable tot that she just might be willing to sacrifice her days of fun and frivolity for a human life of purpose...and love! Visit a world of magic and enchantment in the latest SOULMATES by Donna Clayton.

Even with the help of family and friends, this widower with a twelve-year-old daughter finds it difficult to think about the future—until a woman from his past moves in down the street. Rest and relaxation wouldn't be complete without the laughter and love in *The Daddy's Promise* (SR #1724) by Shirley Jump.

And while away the last of your long summer day with *Make Me a Match* (SR #1725) by Alice Sharpe. A feisty florist, once burned by love, is supposed to be finding a match for her mother and grandmother...not falling for the town's temporary vet! Matchmaking has never been so much fun.

What could be better than greeting summer with beach reading? Enjoy!

Mavis C. Allen
Associate Senior Editor

Please address questions and book requests to:
Silhouette Reader Service
U.S.: 3010 Walden Ave., P.O. Box 1325, Buffalo, NY 14269
Canadian: P.O. Box 609, Fort Erie, Ont. L2A 5X3

Because of Baby

DONNA CLAYTON

Soulmates

SILHOUETTE *Romance*®

Published by Silhouette Books

America's Publisher of Contemporary Romance

This book is dedicated to Cat, Nan, Jeannie, Terry,
Karen, Kathy, Beth, Pam, Carla, Mary, Ruth, Patricia and
Janis; lovers of pixies, one and all! I'd travel
to the ends of the earth for you...or at least to VA.
I love you loopy ladies, you know I do!

 SILHOUETTE BOOKS

ISBN 0-373-19723-3

BECAUSE OF BABY

Copyright © 2004 by Donna Fasano

This edition published by arrangement with Harlequin Books S.A.

® and TM are trademarks of Harlequin Books S.A., used under license.
Trademarks indicated with ® are registered in the United States Patent
and Trademark Office, the Canadian Trade Marks Office and in other
countries.

Visit Silhouette Books at www.eHarlequin.com

Printed in U.S.A.

Books by Donna Clayton

Silhouette Romance

Mountain Laurel #720
Taking Love in Stride #781
Return of the Runaway Bride #999
Wife for a While #1039
Nanny and the Professor #1066
Fortune's Bride #1118
Daddy Down the Aisle #1162
**Miss Maxwell Becomes
    a Mom* #1211
*Nanny in the Nick of Time #1217
**Beauty and the Bachelor
    Dad* #1223
*†The Stand-By Significant
    Other* #1284
*†Who's the Father of Jenny's
    Baby?* #1302
The Boss and the Beauty #1342

His Ten-Year-Old Secret #1373
Her Dream Come True #1399
Adopted Dad #1417
His Wild Young Bride #1441
**The Nanny Proposal #1477
***The Doctor's Medicine
    Woman* #1483
**Rachel and the M.D. #1489
Who Will Father My Baby? #1507
In Pursuit of a Princess #1582
*††The Sheriff's 6-Year-Old
    Secret* #1623
*††The Doctor's Pregnant
    Proposal* #1635
††Thunder in the Night #1647
The Nanny's Plan #1701
Because of Baby #1723

Silhouette Books

The Coltons
Close Proximity

*The Single Daddy Club
†Mother & Child
**Single Doctor Dads
††The Thunder Clan

DONNA CLAYTON

is the recipient of the Diamond Author Award For Literary Achievement 2000 as well as two Holt Medallions. In her opinion, love *is* what makes the world go 'round. She takes great pride in knowing that, through her work, she provides her readers the chance to indulge in some purely selfish romantic entertainment.

One of her favorite pastimes is traveling. Her other interests include walking, reading, visiting with friends, teaching Sunday school, cooking and baking, and she still collects cookbooks, too. In fact, her house is overrun with them.

Please write to Donna c/o Silhouette Books. She'd love to hear from you!

PIXIE RULES AND REGULATIONS

* Savor Every Adventure!

* The Simplest Solution Is Always Best.

* Never Worry, Never Fear. Troubling Thoughts Only Bring Strife.

* Listen To Your Heart To Guide You Toward What Is Right.

* Stay Far Away From Humans. They're Nothing But Trouble.

* Falling In Love With A Human Is Strictly Forbidden!

Prologue

"Quit your messin' about in there, Fern!"

"Trouble's brewin'. I can feel it."

"Leave me be." Fern waved off the warnings called from the open window of the nursery. She cocked her wings at just the right angle and spiraled into a jaunty somersault that elicited a delighted giggle from the tawny-haired baby in the crib. The child would be taken far from Ireland this morning, and Fern was determined to spend every available second with little Katy.

Just being this close to a human was frowned upon in Sidhe—the Irish fairy world. Actually interacting with the baby—entertaining her with fancy flying maneuvers, whispering rhymes that made her giggle—was strictly against the rules.

But Fern simply couldn't resist. Babes, and even tots, were pure, their thoughts and perceptions as yet untainted by worldly matters. Because of this, they had no reason not to believe that fairies did exist. Katy's innocence enabled her to see Fern.

Katy was an extra special baby. Fern took a nose-dive and stopped short to plant a sweet kiss on a cheek that was rose-petal soft, then she zipped into the air and spun around to gaze into a pair of wide eyes that glistened with clever imagination. Ah, yes, Katy was just as special as her mother had been.

Ah, Maire. Katy's mother had been the light of Fern's life for years. Fern had risked ridicule and chastisement from everyone in Sidhe by befriending Maire. But Fern hadn't cared.

However, Maire was gone. Long ago she'd left for a place called America. She'd returned sometime later with a husband in tow. An intriguing man with a mesmerizing mahogany gaze. Fern had understood completely how Maire had lost her heart to Paul Roland. Why, Fern herself would have fallen silk booties over wings for him had such a thing not been forbidden to her.

The last time Maire had returned home, her belly had grown round, and Fern had overheard the humans talk about a baby that was soon to arrive.

This year, however, Paul had returned to Ireland without Maire, and Fern had met Katy for the very first time. Fern had wondered about Maire's absence, but playing with the babe was much more fun than fretting about the unknown. Pixies did their best not to do much worrying.

"He's coming! Fern, get out of there. Now!"

Looking toward the door, Fern smiled when she saw Paul Roland. Her wings hummed like summer lightning and her skin felt prickly. He was the most striking creature—human or otherwise—that she'd ever laid eyes on.

"Fern!"

She tossed her friends an irritated glance. "Sure, he can't see me. He's no believer. I'm perfectly safe."

If the truth be told, Fern had lingered with Katy today because of Paul. She'd said her goodbyes to the baby; however, she longed for the chance to wish him farewell, too. Harboring this fondness for the oh-so-handsome human was dangerous, she knew. But he was going far away today and who knew when she'd see him again.

"Hey, there, sweetie," he crooned to his daughter.

Like warm velvet, his voice was, and it made Fern sigh.

"It's time for us to go." He reached into the crib, and Fern fluttered toward the foot of the bed. He set Katy up on her bottom.

"Da-da," the toddler grinned. "Go bye-bye?"

"Yes, we're going bye-bye, Katy. This visit with grandma and grandpa has been wonderful, but we have to go home. We have to get you ready."

Fern flew to the best vantage point from which to feast on his dark, enchanting eyes. She was close enough to Katy to smell her baby-powder scent, while one of the child's whispery ringlets curled around Fern's ankle. Paul looked away long enough to reach for the white sweater draped over the crib rail.

But quickly his attention was directed back toward Katy again. Even though he couldn't actually see her, Fern felt all warm and happy inside, like she did every morning when she watched the sun climb over the horizon of Sidhe to chase away the cool Irish mist.

"Come on, now," Paul coaxed his daughter. "Let's put this on. It's chilly outside."

"No!" Katy hugged her arms close to her chest.

A silent chuckle erupted from Fern's throat. She'd watched father and daughter play this game often over the past couple of weeks. The routine clearly amused Paul, and laughter rumbled from deep in his chest.

She became so transfixed on his face that she was barely aware of the way in which he and Katy frolicked and fussed until Paul managed to slip one sleeve up his daughter's arm.

Oh, by me heart. Fern silently swore the age-old fairy oath without thought. How she would miss him. She'd miss the silken timbre of his voice, his heated, soapy scent, that quick smile...and those...amazing... arresting eyes.

"Wady go bye-bye!"

As Katy uttered the words, her chubby fist closed around Fern. The toddler's fingers curled tight, and everything went dark in Fern's world. Panic had her gasping in a lungful of air.

"Lady?" Paul's tone held a measure of both amusement and curiosity. "Oh, you are my little lady." He chuckled as he pulled the knitted fabric over the dimpled hand that trapped Fern. Katy's grip loosened and Fern found herself rolling, dragged along by the nappy knit, up, up, until she was lodged in the crook of the child's elbow.

Fern felt herself being hoisted up into the air. Her heart was hammering, but she was pinned, good and firm, between the sweater sleeve and Katy's downy skin.

"Me and my little lady are off to the airport," Paul

said. "We'll be back in America before you can say lickety-split."

"Icky-spit!" Katy gleefully parroted.

Fern could hear her pixie friends buzzing fran tically outside the nursery window, and she could only imagine their horrified expressions as she was whisked away.

Chapter One

Trapped!

For what seemed an eternity, Fern squirmed and wriggled in an attempt to free herself, but it had soon become clear that there was no escape. So, like any good pixie, she settled on the notion of relaxing and simply savoring the adventure...the supreme of all fairy mottos.

Adventure was what she was headed for, that was for sure.

The first leg of the journey had been made in what she'd assumed was an automobile. She'd never been inside of one, but the gentle rocking had lulled Katy to sleep, and Fern had simply enjoyed the soft music that had filled the air and the soft sound of Paul humming along.

Then things had gotten a bit more bumpy as Paul had carried his daughter—and her pixie tag-along—through what Fern could only envision as a huge crowd of humans. There had been some waiting, and then they'd been on the move again. Bumping and jostling down what felt like a narrow corridor...and the clamor of all those voices! Why, Fern easily imagined a thousand different conversations taking place at once.

Finally they'd settled into a seat, and someone helped Paul with something called an extension seat belt meant to fit around both father and daughter.

Fern had suffered a moment or two of anxiety when a din the likes of which she'd never heard set Katy to crying. Whatever it was that surrounded them began to shudder as it shot forward in a flash. Paul's rich voice murmured comforting words that settled Fern—if not Katy—right down. If he wasn't alarmed, she needn't be. Soon the violent vibrating ceased. Fern's ears began to pop, and she knew they were airborne. She and the other pixies had often marveled at those shiny crafts that soared through the sky over Sidhe, and she was awed to think that she was now inside one of them. Yes, she was most definitely going to savor this exciting escapade.

But as time passed, her muscles began to grow stiff. A crick pained her neck and her left foot fell asleep. Katy had been fidgeting for some time, despite Paul's efforts to entertain her. The more the toddler squirmed, the higher her body temperature rose, and Fern became overheated herself. Her wings felt limp and her head was woozy.

Salvation came when Katy shrugged her shoulders, tugged at her sweater and whined, "Me hot, Da-da."

Sweeter words had never been spoken. But Fern hadn't anticipated the force with which she'd be thrust from her cottony trap. She was sent rolling and tumbling, and then she was freefalling. Disoriented, she relaxed into the plummet and then shook out her wings by sheer instinct. She landed with a double skip on Paul's knee. Stretching this way and that, she worked the kinks from her aching muscles.

Katy began to whimper.

"How about a drink of apple juice?" Paul asked.

The child's snivels progressed to chin-trembling tears. He pulled out the lidded cup, his arm jerked, and a drip of juice sloshed onto his hand. Realizing that she was parched herself, Fern zipped into the air high enough that she could bend over and sip the sweet nectar from his skin.

Sensing Paul's sudden stillness, Fern turned to look up at him. His dark eyes seemed to be directed right at her, and every inch of her neck and arms sparkled as though pointed stars rolled end over end along her flesh. Her lips formed a silent oh. Did he see her?

But the question barely had time to form in her mind before he blinked a couple of times, then picked up his crying daughter. "You're tired, sweetie. Let's go change your diaper and then you can take a nap."

Fern followed close behind them. In the tiny cubicle, Paul changed Katy's diaper, but the toddler continued to fuss. He tried to soothe her, but Fern could see that, tired himself, he was becoming flustered.

Hoping to cause a diversion, Fern lit into the air and whooshed back and forth in front of Katy's face. But to no avail.

"Come on," Paul murmured. "You need a rest."

He left the rest room, and the door latched shut

before Fern could escape. She was trapped once again.

Landing on a small ledge by the entrance, she waited. Someone would come in soon enough and she'd be free.

She frowned when she thought of how her attempt to distract the toddler from her sobs had been unsuccessful. Fern didn't like to fail. Paul had been tense. How she wished she could help.

If she were human she could help.

What a scandalous thought. Talk about breaking the rules! Human transformation was the most prohibited of all pixie policies. Why, she could be tossed out of Sidhe altogether.

Paul's exhausted face floated into her mind, his dark gaze weary with frustration.

She'd heard of rebel fairies turning into foxes or hares for a short time so they could race and play with their forest friends. But to turn human? She'd be the shame of every pixie in Ireland.

But she wasn't in Ireland any longer, was she?

Closing her eyes, she pictured herself rocking wee Katy to sleep. Then the image softened and she was smoothing the frown from Paul's troubled brow. She sighed. She could be of help to him…she could…

Fern lifted her eyelids and found herself staring into the mirror—*at her own human reflection!*

Paul had done everything he could think of to calm his daughter. He'd allowed her to grow overly tired, and if there was one thing he'd learned over the past twenty-four months of being Katy's daddy, of raising her single-handedly, it was that that was *never* a good thing.

He'd plied her with every toy he'd brought along, terribly grateful for the empty seats on either side of him that the partially filled flight had provided and on which were now strewn an array of stuffed animals, rattles and playthings. Now, though, he hummed and rocked, but it seemed that all Katy wanted to do was fight him and the slumber she so desperately needed. Why did return transatlantic flights always seem longer than the ones that whisked you away from home?

The question barely had time to fade from his thoughts when the most peculiar pair of shiny satin slippers came into his view. The toes were turned up just slightly, lending them an almost enchanted charm. Paul smiled in spite of himself.

His gaze lifted to a pair of delicate ankles, then further over shapely calves and twin creamy, firm thighs that disappeared beneath the hem of a royal blue dress. With hips that had just the right swell, a waist narrow enough for him to span with both his hands and breasts that were nicely rounded, the woman standing before him was…well, Paul estimated, she was a perfect example of the female persuasion.

When he looked into her face, things only got better. Vibrant blue-green eyes flashed with liveliness, her pert nose was cute and her hair was a mass of coppery curls that just brushed the tops of her sun-kissed shoulders.

It was crazy, but it seemed as if she radiated a muted glow…a humming energy just waiting to spring from its boundaries the first chance it got. He was momentarily spellbound.

Her bronzed shoulders rounded rather coyly. "I'm here ta help."

The quiet resonance of her voice was comforting, and her soft brogue clearly pegged her as Irish.

Evidence of the gratitude washing through him showed in the small smile he offered her. "Thanks," he said, "but my Katy's too cranky for anyone to have to deal with at the moment. Even I can't make her happy, it seems."

However, rather than nodding and backing away as he'd expected her to do, the woman began clearing the aisle seat of the teddy bear and plastic stacking toys that riddled it.

"Nonsense." In a move that could only be described as graceful, she eased down beside him.

The fabric of her dress made a slight brushing sound as her fanny slid against the cushion, and the fact that he was aware of her enough to notice shocked him.

"Give her here," she ordered. "I just love babes."

Obviously, the woman didn't have a clue about children. There was no way Katy was going to allow herself to be held by a stranger, not when irritability and exhaustion had her so cantankerous.

"But you don't understand—"

Ignoring him, the woman reached out and tenderly touched his daughter's arm. "How's me pretty Katy?"

Paul expected his daughter to howl, but Katy left him stupefied when she looked at the woman through bleary eyes, and said through hiccupping sobs, "My wady,'' as if an angelic savior had appeared right out of the clouds.

Katy scrambled from his lap, shoving herself away from him and launching herself into the arms of the stranger.

The woman's light laughter rang like musical notes as she pulled the toddler to her. She didn't seem the least bit fazed when Katy decided to get right up in her face, smooth both hands down her cheeks and gaze deeply into her eyes. It seemed Katy was mesmerized, and Paul grinned, thinking that he'd had the same initial reaction to the woman.

"Wady,'' Katy whispered in wonder. Her small mouth pulled into a smile even as the last of her fat tears were rolling from her big dark eyes.

Paul's amazement only grew when his daughter snuggled down into the cradle provided by the woman's arms. Katy's eyelids immediately fluttered closed, and she went still.

"I don't believe it,'' he murmured. "I just don't believe it.''

The woman only smiled.

"I'm Paul,'' he introduced himself. It was simply out of habit that he didn't offer his last name. When people discovered his identity, they all too often tended to act a little strange. Effusive and fussy. Paul avoided that as much as possible, just as he avoided the pretensions of limos and first-class accommodations. He liked to think of himself as a regular Joe, just like 99.9 percent of everyone else on earth.

"I'm Fern,'' she supplied.

Nice name. The opinion whispered through his head from somewhere in the back of his brain. And completely appropriate, he determined. She had the same litheness and grace as the flowing branches of a fern.

He blinked. It had been a long while since his thinking had taken such a whimsical turn. When he composed his stories, that kind of habitual imagery and quirky reflection had been imperative to his work, but it had been two long years since he'd put a single creative thought to paper. He'd been too busy with real life.

"So, Fern—" suddenly he felt tongue-tied, like an awkward teen trying to break the ice "—you're on your way to the States?"

"I'm going to America."

The inflection in her voice almost gave the impression she didn't know that the two places were one and the same, but that would be rather silly. Everyone knew...

He shoved the notion out of his head and asked, "Is this your first trip abroad?"

She nodded. "It is."

"So, you're excited." It wasn't a question. He could clearly see the thrill gleaming in her turquoise gaze, and it only made her more beautiful.

If that were possible.

Her smile widened, and that's when he learned that the concept of her becoming more beautiful *was* possible, and all it had taken was a smile.

"I am that."

The words came out sounding like, *I yem,* and Paul suppressed the pleasurable smile that threatened to curl his lips. He liked her accent.

Then she added, "I've never been so excited in me life."

He chuckled. "I can understand. The first time I visited Ireland, I wanted to see and do everything."

"That's the spirit. Savor the adventure." Her head bobbed twice, the movement sending her curls bouncing. "Now, those words are good ones to live by."

"They are," he agreed. "Is this trip for pleasure? Or are you going for a job?"

"I don't do anything unless there's pleasure involved."

Her pointed expression had him going still. For an instant he thought she might be flirting with him, teasing him with a subtle sensual innuendo. But he realized quickly enough that there was no guile in her expression, just as there was none intended in her declaration. In fact, he realized, she was expressing herself simply and honestly, and that was refreshing, indeed.

"I have no idea about a job." One of her shoulders raised a fraction. "But finding one would probably be important, I would expect. And the experience might be fun."

"Are you staying with family? Or friends?" He shouldn't be poking his nose in her business, but he couldn't help himself. Curiosity simmered in him like a pot of water on a burner.

"No. I know no one in America." She paused. "Except you and Katy, that is."

Something stirred inside him, spiraling and twisting to life.

Her gaze dipped. "Sounds like you're thinkin' I

have a plan. I have to admit, I don't have one. It's impossible to plan an adventure, you know."

The warmth that had curled deep in his belly was completely forgotten. No plan? She was just going to step off the plane in New York and walk out into the unknown? He was hit with what felt like a dozen questions that needed asking. Did she have hotel reservations? Did she have enough money? Did she know it wasn't safe for a woman traveling alone? Did she have an emergency contact? How would she—

"I'll be fine. I always am."

The concern that rushed at him must have shown itself on his face if she felt the need to assure him. But her sweet innocence ignited in him a powerful urge to protect.

Her blue-green eyes leveled on his face. "I think it's time you told me a little something about you."

So that ingenuous charm was balanced with a touch of brass. He liked that.

"All you've said was that you were eager to see everything in Ireland the first time you visited. So...have you? Seen everythin', I mean?"

He couldn't get over the way her brilliant eyes sparkled, seeming to draw him in, luring him to reveal all his secrets. He shook the ridiculous idea out of his head.

He pondered her question for only a moment before all the implications of it had him wincing slightly. "The circumstances between my first visits to your beautiful country and this one were...well, quite different, to say the least."

She remained silent, evidently waiting for him to expound further.

"I honeymooned in Ireland during my first visit," he told her. Memories of Maire threatened, but he held them at bay. Now wasn't the time to be swallowed up by those shadows.

"How lovely. You must have had a grand time of it."

"We did. And our second trip was just as wonderful. Maire and I had the pleasure of announcing to her parents that we were going to have a baby. Well, we didn't really have to announce the fact, all they had to do was take one look at her."

Memories loomed and threatened to swamp him. He took a head-clearing breath. Leaving the past in the past, he rushed ahead to the present. "But this trip, it was just me and Katy. You see, my wife, Maire, died giving birth to our daughter. She experienced some unexpected complications that the doctors hadn't foreseen. That they hadn't been prepared for. None of us were prepared." He was vaguely aware of the far-off inflection his voice had taken on. He cleared his throat. "That was two years ago."

But the void inside stubbornly remains, the words echoed silently.

With nothing short of brute force, he pulled himself back to the conversation at hand. "Anyway, with Katy being a baby and all, it had been impossible for me to take her back to Ireland until now." Paul wondered why he was being so free with such personal information. This was so unlike him, yet it just felt right. "Her grandparents had come to visit her, of course, but I want Katy to be familiar with the place where her mother grew up—"

His gaze latched on to Fern's face, the sight of her

mournful gaze cutting his thought clean in two. Sadness seemed to pulse from her, and her eyes glistened with unshed tears.

Warmth permeated every nook and cranny in his being. She was a person of great compassion, a woman with an empathetic heart.

"Hey, now, stop that." He reached over and smoothed his palm along her forearm. The instant his fingertips contacted her flesh, the intention of comforting the woe she was experiencing on his behalf left his mind as if it had never been there.

Her skin was smooth, the heat of her startling.

Paul pulled his hand away, the topic of the discussion and the delight shooting through him being so at odds that it set off a twinge of guilt that filled him with confusion.

Clearly, what he'd revealed had affected Fern. Careful not to touch her the way his subconscious was willing him to do, he murmured, "That all happened a long time ago. Katy and I are doing okay. Really. We are."

She didn't look convinced. But then, Paul didn't see how his pronouncement should persuade her one way or the other when it hadn't done much to influence him over these many long and lonely months.

Verbal affirmations were great, but how did you go about filling up the holes that were left after tragedy plundered your soul?

Since glancing into that mirror and seeing herself in real flesh-and-blood human form, Fern felt as if every sensation, every emotion, had been magnified a hundredfold.

She couldn't say just how she'd transformed into a human. The experience was brand new to her. She was aware, however, that she was breaking a major pixie rule, and if she let herself dwell on that fact, she'd go into a panic for sure. So…Fern simply decided not to dwell on the hard truth. At least, not right now. Not when she was so focused on Paul.

She'd already admitted that Paul was as comely a creature as had ever had the fortune to live; however, when she'd walked the length of the aisle to where he sat and gazed down upon him, why, every inch of her skin had seemed to come alive with an awareness she'd never experienced before. And when he'd cast those mahogany eyes on her, she'd thought her knees would give way then and there.

What she might say to him had never entered her head until she was facing him. It was too late then to ponder in depth the follies of telling him the truth about herself. The last thing she wanted was for him to think she was some crazy pixie—insane person, in his view—who had come to vex him. It had only taken a fraction of an instant to make her mind up that acting a stranger was for the best. Besides, she hadn't formally made his acquaintance before that moment, now, had she?

Fern had had to practically bully her way into the seat beside him, which had been quite rude, she knew, even by pixie standards. But if she hadn't sat down she'd have risked succumbing to the faintness that had been swimming in her head.

Her heart had nearly ripped in two with tenderness when she'd held Katy for the first time. Oh, the affection she'd felt for the bairn when they had laughed together in the nursery back in Ireland had been great. But something about holding the toddler in her arms filled her with overwhelming feelings that were both unimaginable and breathtaking.

But the most jarring commotion she'd had to endure had been the impact of learning that Maire had died. Grief had walloped her from all sides. Anguish had scalded her eye sockets and burned the back of her throat.

It wasn't as if she had never felt sadness before. Bad things happened in Sidhe, certainly. But it was the fairy way to avoid misfortune and bad dealings. A pixie spent her days frolicking and flying and having fun.

The sorrow that swept through her now, though, couldn't be avoided by merely winging away from the moment.

Although Paul's touch had calmed her angst, it had churned up other—very peculiar—emotions. She'd flushed with an odd heat, and a strange feeling had knotted in her belly.

Fern had no idea what was happening to her in this new human body, all she knew was that she liked the warmth and smoothness of Paul's skin against her own. When he'd withdrawn his hand from her arm, she'd suffered something similar to acute desolation.

Human emotions, she was quickly discovering, were awesome in their power.

"Let's talk about something a little more pleasant," Paul suggested.

His intent was to chase away the gloom that had settled around them, she suspected. Although her smile was quivery, she nodded in emphatic agreement.

"What can I tell you about myself? Hmm..."

The rumbling resonance that rose from his chest as he pondered allowed Fern to let go of her sorrow over Maire. *By me heart.* The silent oath echoed in her head, but the very sound of the man's voice was enough to make her forget the rest of the whole wide world.

"Katy and I live just outside New York City in the house I was raised in. My father ran a horse farm."

"I love horses. Where I come from they're considered one of the noblest of beasts."

"Well, the horses are gone now." He absently ran his fingertips along the armrest. "Once Dad died, Mom couldn't run the business by herself. Running the farm hadn't ever interested me. I had no talent with horseflesh, anyway. Working and communicating with animals is a gift...a gift that I wasn't blessed with. So the horses were sold to other breeders."

Fern knew that work—or an occupation, as she'd heard it called—was very important to humans. She'd witnessed people in Ireland going out to toil in the fields or going off to factories or working in the shops. Labor seemed to be a defining aspect in their existence. Hadn't that been one of Paul's first questions to her? So she asked him about his job.

"I'm a writer," he supplied. "A novelist."

She knew of books, and was even known to fly through the small village library on a dare. Her friends would laugh in delight when she'd use her magic dust to knock a book to the floor and startle someone, or she'd flutter her wings ferociously in or-

der to turn the pages of this book or that to the vex-
ation of the librarian. The harmless pranks were all
in fun, of course. A good pixie made it a habit to be
helpful and kind, but even respectable pixies suffered
with boredom every so often.

"So you're a teller of tall tales?"

He grinned, and Fern's insides twisted up.

He said, "Horror stories are my forte."

"Ah—" she offered him a knowing nod "—you
like to frighten small children."

Paul laughed. "Actually, my work is geared to
adults."

Her eyes widened. "Your stuff must be good and
gory, then."

The sigh issuing from him conveyed a weariness
that made her head cock to the side. He evidently
sensed her curiosity.

"I haven't written anything for quite some time."

Ever since Maire's passing. He didn't have to say
the words. Fern just somehow knew it as fact. Em-
pathy rose like floodwaters. Had she not been holding
the sleeping Katy in her arms, she'd have reached out
to him. The urge to comfort him was intense. Again
she realized that the magnitude of these human emotions pulsing through her was like nothing she'd ever
endured.

"But that's got to change," he told her. "My publisher's been after me. They want a book, and they
want it soon."

"They've got confidence in you, then."

"What do you mean?" His question was asked in
a feathery whisper.

"If this publisher—" she wasn't certain what a

publisher was, but she wasn't so daft that she couldn't figure out it had something to do with the book-making business ''—thought you weren't capable of the job, he'd have called someone else.''

Paul studied her face for a moment, and then Fern saw his deportment change right before her very eyes; his spine straightened, his shoulders leveled and his gaze brightened.

''Thank you, Fern. I guess I needed to have that pointed out.''

Again he sighed. But this time the sound of it was easier, less tense.

Pleasure caused her toes to curl inside her silk booties. The fact that she'd lifted his spirits filled her with a delight that was absolute. Total. Oh, she wouldn't mind basking in this warmth for a good long time.

''Of course,'' he murmured, ''there are some problems that need to be worked out. Like Katy.''

It was almost as if his discussion turned inward, as if the chat had turned serious and he was the only one participating.

''I guess I could write while she's sleeping. But I can't always count on the muse to come when I call. There's day care, of course. I'm sure I could find a reputable—''

His sentence stopped short. Then his gaze swung to her face. It was evident that he'd been struck with some amazing thought or other.

''Fern, you said you need to look for a job. You said you don't have a place to stay. We could help each other, you and I.''

If she could continue to be of some service to him, that would make her very happy.

"After seeing you with Katy, this is probably a silly question," he said. "But I have to ask. Do you have experience with children?"

"I *love* children! I spend most of me time entertaining the little tykes, I do."

He smiled. "I could tell pretty quickly that you have a way with kids. Katy fell for your charms from the get-go."

"She's a sweet thing, Katy is."

"So would you consider it?" he asked. "Would you come stay with me and Katy? Take care of her for a fair wage and a place to stay? I'd have to check your references, but—"

Dread forced Fern's eyes closed. Please don't check me references. There are no references to check. I'm good and kind, and I love sweet Katy.

"But I really don't need to do that," Paul said, his voice suddenly soft and fuzzy. "I can tell you're good and kind, and it's clear that Katy trusts you. I should, too."

Fern's eyes went wide. It was as if her very thoughts had the power of pixie magic. She didn't know how it had happened, or if it would ever happen again. But she was grateful for the enchantment.

"Like I said, I live close to the city," Paul said, his tone miraculously back to normal again. "I promise to show you the sights. When you return to Ireland, you can tell all your friends about the places you've seen."

His dark eyes sparkled with excitement. Exhilaration gathered in Fern's chest and made it hard for her to draw breath.

"Well, now, isn't this turn of events far from what

I was expecting?'' she said, astonished by the winded feeling that had overtaken her. "You make the arrangement sound like an adventure. And, well, a good adventure is just what I'm after.''

Chapter Two

Excitement churned in Fern's stomach until she was faint with it.

Oh, she'd experienced a few anxious moments since discovering her newfound ability to turn into human form. The first had been when she'd noticed how the flight attendant had begun casting suspicious looks her way as she sat rocking the sleeping Katy in the seat next to Paul.

Fern had never been a passenger on an airplane before, but common sense told her that some sort of list or count had to be taken of the travelers. Having someone like herself just appear out of the blue, someone who hadn't boarded the plane when everyone else had, would probably cause quite a ruckus among the airline workers.

When the flight attendant had approached her, telling her the plane would be landing soon and that she should return to her assigned seat, Fern had gently handed Paul's daughter over to him.

With the wary eyes of the flight attendant still on her, Fern's heart had thrashed in her chest when Paul suggested that once they landed they meet up near Baggage Claim, or if they got separated, just outside of "Customs." Fern hadn't a clue what he was talking about or where she might find these places. However, she calmed right down when she decided the simplest solution—another pixie motto—would be to revert to her true pixie self, hide in the safety of Katy's toy sack and have Paul carry her to their meeting spot.

However, she'd then found herself at the back of the cabin and smack-dab in the center of another tense moment when she discovered her power to convert didn't seem to be working. That was the moment she was struck with the realization that the mystical ability of metamorphosis had rules of use. And one of them was that no human eye could witness her gift of transformation.

Fern had slipped into the restroom cubicle. With all the people coming and going, she hadn't worried about propping open the door. Swiftly she found herself winging through the air, light as a feather and fancy-free. Being human, she'd learned, had taken its toll on a body. All that skin and bones and sinew came with a heaviness that had weighed Fern down to the point of exhaustion.

She slipped into the toy sack, snuggled up to Katy's cuddly teddy bear and fell fast asleep. When she awakened, she yawned through a smile, thinking her dream of being human, of spending time holding the baby and chatting with Paul, had been just lovely. But then she became cognizant of the fleecy softness against her cheek, and she looked up to see the brown fuzzy bear staring at her with its button eyes. Fern's gaze widened as she zipped out of the sack and into the air to see where she was and what was happening.

Seeing Paul standing in a wide area waiting with Katy, she searched frantically for a place that would lend her enough privacy to transfigure into a human. A nearby supply closet worked just fine; however, the moment she stepped out into the hallway among all the passersby, she was acutely aware that there was something very different about her attire compared to everyone else's.

While she'd been seated on the plane, she hadn't noticed, but here in the hustle and bustle of the crowd, it was obvious that there was not another soul that she could see who was wearing satin slippers. And not one person's shoes had upturned toes as hers did. The footwear did come in a vast array of styles and colors, though, she saw.

One particular pair worn by a smartly dressed woman caught Fern's eye, and she wished she had shoes like that. Suddenly her feet felt a wee bit cramped. Fern looked down and gasped when she saw an identical pair had taken the place of her booties.

What fun! It seemed her magical powers of changing extended beyond what she'd first imagined.

She waited until Paul was busy with Katy before she approached him, so he wouldn't realize she hadn't come from the direction from which he was expecting her to.

''There y' are!'' she greeted.

Katy squealed with glee and clapped her hands. Paul's handsome face lifted, his frown easing.

"I was beginning to worry..." His sentence faded as he looked down at her empty hands. "Where's your luggage?"

Instantly Fern grasped the idea of what the baggage claim area he spoke of was for. But she was caught now, and hadn't a clue how she could go about explaining herself. No way would he believe the truth, not when she scarcely believed it herself.

"They lost your bags." The irate retort had the crease in his brow deepening. "What a lousy thing to happen." He shifted Katy to his other hip. "So that's where you've been. Filing a report. And here I thought you'd changed your mind about coming to work as Katy's nanny. When do they expect to contact you about your luggage?" He paused. "Fern, how will they know where to send your things?"

The man surely was full of questions. All she could do was lift her hands, palms up. "I'm staying with you, aren't I?" The question was all she had for an answer. Beyond that, she was lost.

"Ah—" he nodded "—smart woman. You gave them my name and they looked me up in the computer. Good thinking."

Clouds of uncertainty threatened to shadow his gaze again, but in the end he evidently let go of whatever thought was niggling at him.

"Well, no sense standing around here all evening," he told her. "If you'll take Katy, I'll get our bags. Thank goodness those made it safely." He handed the gleeful toddler to her. "We're off to find a bus that will take us to long-term parking."

This traveling experience put Fern's senses on overload. She pointed out every interesting thing to

Katy, and the child's eyes just gleamed as if she, too, was encountering all these things for the first time.

"I just can't get over how she's taken to you," Paul murmured as they got off the bus and started across the parking lot.

Fern watched as he loaded the suitcases into the boot of the car, the muscles of his back playing against the cotton fabric of his shirt when he bent over to arrange the bags. A tingling heat permeated her being, and she had to make a conscious effort to inhale and exhale slowly so she wouldn't succumb to the peculiar turmoil racing in her head, in her body. What in the world was this warm and wonderful feeling that pulsed through her like golden, sun-heated nectar?

He buckled Katy into a special seat and they drove out of the garage. Once they were on the road, Fern couldn't believe how the automobiles seemed to fly in all directions.

The city skyline had her sighing in awe.

"There must be a frightful number of people living here if they fill up all of those buildings."

Paul chuckled. "There are an appalling number of people in the city," he agreed. "It must be very different where you're from. Where *are* you from, by the way?"

"Sidhe." The name for her world tumbled from her lips before she could stop it.

"I've never heard of that town," he said.

"Well, it's...very small."

He smiled. "I love those little Irish hamlets. I'm sure Sidhe is just magical."

Fern gazed out at the urban horizon, surprised by

his accurate description. She whispered, "Sidhe truly is a magical place."

"Very different from New York, I'm sure."

She only nodded, unable to find the words to describe just how different their worlds really were. Until today her only goal had been to laugh and enjoy life with her friends in Sidhe. But now she was discovering she had a...

She contemplated how to describe this revelation.

A purpose. That's what it was. A reason for being and doing. Helping Paul with Katy so he could get back to writing. And she liked this brand-new sense of satisfaction filling her. Knowing she had already helped Paul—knowing that she was on her way to continue to do so—saturated her with a contentment of awesome proportion.

Soon the city faded into open spaces, meadows and fields, more reminiscent of what Fern was used to in her homeland. Paul turned onto a tree-lined gravel drive that wound its way to an end in front of a large, white clapboard farmhouse.

Getting out of the car, Fern gazed out at the barns and paddocks, at the wide-open spaces. "This looks like a wonderful place for a boy to grow up."

The rope hanging from the ancient elm in the side yard made her smile. She liked the mental picture that popped into her head of Paul swinging high, the wind blowing through his sandy locks.

"It was." He opened the back door, and after unlatching his daughter from her car seat, he pulled a sleeping Katy into his arms. "If you'll grab her toy sack and the diaper bag, we'll head on inside and put her to bed. She's had an awfully long day. I'll come back later for my bag."

He went up the porch steps and only fumbled a little with his keys before pushing open the door. Fern followed him up the stairway, and when she entered Katy's room, her smile widened.

The walls and ceiling were painted pale blue. Puffy clouds were gathered here and there. A weeping willow tree was sketched in one corner, its leafy branches bending to brush the flowers and mushrooms and tufts of brilliant green grass painted around the bottom of the wall. And magical fairies were everywhere she looked.

One pixie was perched on a cloud. A few more were winging through the sky. Several frolicked among the morning glory vines that twisted and reached upward. Every single one of them expressed an unmistakable joy.

There were elves, too, and gnomes wearing funny hats and expressive faces. One looked centuries old with too many wrinkles to count, yet even he was grinning with happiness.

Bliss exuberated from the fanciful mural.

Although it wasn't the pixie way to worry, Fern had often wondered if Maire had grown up and forgotten the days when they had played and giggled together. When children were babes, it was easy enough for them to see—to believe—that fairies did exist. But the passing of years never failed to dim the memory.

So-called maturity had people accepting nothing but cold, hard fact as reality. When the real truth of the matter was that life contained much that could not be seen with the eye or heard with the ear. However, discernment of the magic in the world required a delighted heart. And clearly, Maire had never completely let go of the blessing that was her childlike enchantment. Fern could feel both the love and the pure and festive energy that had been left behind by Katy's mother.

Paul didn't seem to notice Fern's fascination with the room's decor. He was busy tucking his daughter into her crib.

A flash of gleaming copper caught her eye and had her crossing the carpet toward the crib for a closer look. There among the willow branches was a pixie that was the very image of herself right down to the fiery curls and the blue dress and boots.

"By me heart," she breathed. "I can't believe it."

"What's wrong?"

She whirled to see Paul studying her.

"You look upset," he said.

"No," she assured him. "Not upset. Not at all." She gazed around her. "The room is just lovely, Paul."

He smiled, and Fern's insides warmed deliciously.

"Maire had a fondness for all sorts of imps and gnomes and pixies." Affection softened his smile. "There was an innocence about her, Fern. And it showed in her art."

"She was a professional artist?"

He nodded. "She tried her hand at everything. Sculpting. Drawing. But painting was in her blood." His mouth quirked. "Just like sprites and elves were."

Fern's gaze swept the room. "She was gifted."

"She often worked as an illustrator for children's books. And she had a picture book of her work published. It was called *Pixie Pleasures.*"

A chuckle bubbled up from Fern's throat. "Wonderful! I'd love to see it."

He went to the shelves, pulled out a book and handed it to her.

Fern lifted the cover. The bright, shiny pages were meant to make the reader smile, and she did just that. "It's beautiful." She turned one page, then another. "Just beautiful."

"Maire was a talented woman."

Closing the book, Fern smoothed her hand over the jacket. It was as if she were touching a piece of Maire, and that gave her a cozy feeling.

She looked up at Paul and found him studying her.

"There was something…magic about my wife. Something…enchanted."

He seemed to hover on the brink of hesitation, as if he wasn't sure he should verbalize the thoughts crowding his mind.

Finally he said, "I get that same feeling from you. That same…vibrancy."

Heat suffused Fern's cheeks, and she wanted to lower her eyes from his, but she was determined not to. Something was happening. Something she didn't dare miss.

The room grew still…and warm…and uncomfortably close. The air seemed to thicken all around her until she thought she may not be able to draw a breath. Her heart fluttered. Her pulse raced. A vague feeling…a wanting…an unexplainable yearning… swirled inside her like smoky tendrils. The only feeling she could compare it to was when she was terribly, terribly famished. Yet this had nothing to do with hunger for food.

This was the strangest and most powerful experience she'd had yet since transforming into a human. The significance of the emotion was almost frightening, but for the life of her, she didn't have any idea what it was all about.

Whatever it was, however, Paul was sensing it, too.

His gaze had gone all smudgy with shadows. His jaw tensed. And it seemed as if he barely breathed. Fern guessed he sensed the thickness of the air just as she had.

He inched toward her, and she hoped with all her might that he'd touch her again as he had on the airplane. To feel his skin against her, the heat of him on her, just might quench this peculiar wanting that pulsed from her very soul.

However, rather than reaching out for her, his hand lowered to grasp the picture book. He slid it from her hands.

"I'm sorry, Fern. I'm terribly sorry."

Remorse encrusted his words, and before she could ask why he was looking so guilt-ridden, he turned from her. He shoved the book back into the slot on the shelf and then bolted for the door.

He stopped at the threshold and twisted to face her. "You can take the room next door. The bathroom is at the end of the hall. Go and freshen up. I'll get my bag out of the car and then rustle us up something to eat."

He was gone, and she was left with a distinctive resonance...an almost haunting ache that, although it was fading with each second that ticked by, she feared would never completely vanish.

Then panic set in as she worried she might never experience it again.

The following morning Fern awoke in the guest room curled up in the center of her luxurious down pillow. She stretched her arms and unfurled her wings. The first flight of the day was always the best, in her opinion, for it was then that she was reminded how wonderful and carefree life was. That was what a proper pixie lived for—happy-go-lucky days.

After several joyous and perfectly executed spins, she landed on the windowsill and looked out at the day. The sun shone bright, and the crystalline sky was clear but for a few fluffy clouds. Adventure was in the air. She could feel it.

The time she'd spent with Paul last night had been both exhilarating and difficult. He'd fixed them cheese omelettes and buttered toast, and Fern had loved the sharp taste of the gooey cheddar. However, there had been a tenseness between them. Had it been a lute string, she could have plucked it and made it twang.

Fern had realized that the awkwardness had had something to do with the potent energy that had hummed around them in Katy's room just before he'd apologized and fled. The remorse that had clouded his gaze just before he left her had been involved, too. But Fern hadn't been able to sort it out completely.

They had talked about what would be expected of her during her stay. Paul told her his only expectation was that she mind his daughter. She needn't cook or worry about household chores. Fern had been relieved because she'd never used a stove before. Pixies survived on berries and nuts and flower nectar, just like all the other wild woodland creatures.

Fern flitted from the windowsill now, landing on the center of the mattress, her thoughts still trapped in her memories of last night.

The topic of the evening's conversation had turned to her when he'd asked her more about her life in Ireland. Mainly it was her career he'd been curious about.

"You said you've worked with children." Although he hadn't posed his words as a question, he wanted answers, that much had been obvious to her.

Her smile had belied the mild fretful feeling inside her. She hadn't worked for wages a single day of her life. "There is nothing quite like the happy face of a child, and I always do all I can to make 'em laugh."

Paul hadn't seemed quite satisfied with that answer.

"Well, did you work in private homes, as a sitter? A nanny? Or did you work at a child-care facility?"

"I've always gone wherever the children are."

She hadn't been lying, really. She'd simply been evading the truth by avoiding the details.

She'd cocked her head a fraction. "It's funny," she told him, "I've always had this sense with little ones. I always know when I'm needed. Like on that airplane with Katy. I just knew you needed my help." She had chuckled and honestly admitted, "Of course, I never imagined my offer would lead me to this point, but—"

He had reached for her then, his warm fingers sliding over her hand, and he'd given it a gentle squeeze. "I am glad you're here, Fern."

The sense that he was trying to convey some unspoken message had been strong. Yet there had also been a cautious hesitancy in his touch. Again she simply hadn't been able to put all the pieces together to form a complete picture.

After their late meal Paul had claimed fatigue, and they'd both headed off to their prospective rooms to sleep.

The morning sun streaming through the window warmed her. Fern smoothed her hands over her knees and saw that she'd become human. The realization startled her a bit because—just like her initial transformation on the plane—she hadn't been cognizant of the actual change.

She stood and glanced at her reflection in the mirror that hung above the bureau. Her blue dress was terribly rumpled. Absently she looked down at her bare feet.

The sandals she'd been wearing last night still sat just inside the bedroom door where she'd left them. Her mind began to churn. If she could magically conjure shoes for her feet, why not clothes for her body?

A magazine sat on the table next to the bed. She flipped through the pages looking for an appropriate outfit. She wanted something comfortable, that was for sure. But she wanted something that looked good, too. She might be a fairy, but she was still female, and every female wanted to be pleasing to the eye.

Fern flipped another glossy page, refusing to ponder too long on why looking attractive seemed so im-

portant all of a sudden. Instead she studied the images
of the women in the magazine.

She ran her finger down the length of a beautiful
black dress, and before she had time to fully inhale,
she saw that her blue shift had been replaced by the
image she'd been studying. Fern smiled, turning her
body this way and that to make the hem flip and
dance.

The black high-heeled shoes made her legs look
even longer, and she decided she liked this outfit quite
a lot.

However, when she looked back at the picture, she
noticed the wording described "elegant evening attire." Common sense told her a woman would only
wear evening clothes in the evening.

Thoughts churned in her head. Those sandals still
sat by the door, yet her rumpled blue dress was gone.
She took a quick peek down the neck of the fancy
black dress just to be sure. Yep, her shift had disappeared, too.

Fern decided a test of her powers was in order. She
tugged the black dress off her body, and after a little
fumbling, unlatched the strange stretchy, constricting
garment that bound her breasts and finally peeled off
the satiny slip of fabric covering her private bits. She
wondered if she could conjure up a new outfit and
keep the fancy black evening dress.

A woman in the magazine wearing a simple skirt
and top and some plain, rubber-soled shoes caught her
gaze. Perfect!

In the blink of an eye, she was wearing the skirt,
top and white shoes. And, lo and behold, the black

dress and underthings were still on the bed where she'd tossed them.

How fun was this?

"Fern, me girl," she murmured to her grinning reflection, "at this rate you could open a boutique. You could be rich."

She would do no such thing, of course. Conjuring clothing magically and then selling them for profit would be wrong. Some whispery echo coming from her heart told her so.

Besides, she didn't know how long the magic would last. The fabric of the skirt and top was real enough, all right, but she had no idea if or when the charm might end and the clothes might disappear—

The thought made her blanch. What if her ability to become human just disappeared suddenly? How would she help Paul if she wasn't in this form?

The notion so troubled her that she shoved it right out of her brain.

After a quick stop at the bathroom to take care of her ablutions, she peeked into Katy's room and saw that the toddler's crib was empty. Paul's bedroom door was open, and his bed, too, was empty. So she went down the stairs to look for them.

The house was still, so Fern found her way to the kitchen. She sniffed the pot of brown liquid, the acrid scent making her nose wrinkle with distaste. Then she opened the refrigerator and pulled out some fruit juice. She was sipping the luscious liquid when Paul entered the house through the kitchen door.

"Hi," he said. Katy was hoisted in one arm, and he carried a plastic cage-like contraption by a handle in his other hand.

"Good morning." Just seeing his handsome face made her heart *ka-chunk* behind her ribs. Fern's gaze shifted to the child. "Hi, there, Katy-loo."

Katy grinned and waved and reached out her arms for Fern to take her. Fern did just that.

"We went to pick up Fluffy," Paul said.

He set the cage down on the floor and opened the door. Out walked the fattest tabby cat that Fern had ever seen.

"Now, aren't you a gorgeous creature?" Fern bent down and Fluffy strolled leisurely over to offer her the chance to pet him as if such an occasion was a rare privilege.

"Fwuffy!" Katy cried, reaching out for the feline. Fern set her down on the floor so she could stroke the cat's soft fur.

"Katy was up at the crack of dawn," Paul said. "And I knew the boarding facility opened early, so we slipped off to pick up Fluffy. I wanted to give you the opportunity to sleep in, to acclimatize yourself to the time change."

His gaze was easy, and there didn't seem to be any tension in him. She was glad. She didn't like the idea that the awkwardness they had waded through last night would taint their every moment together.

"Did you sleep well?"

She nodded. "I did, thanks. And yerself?"

"I'm all rested up and ready to start back to work." Excitement seemed to vibrate off him in waves. "I'm really looking forward to sitting down at my computer. I haven't felt like this in a long time."

Her smile widened, and she recognized the warmth flowing through her as contentment. He could work because she was here to care for his daughter. That was such a gratifying thought.

However, she'd barely had time enough to bask in the wonderful feeling when a frown pinched his brow as his eyes raked down and then back up the length of her. He pointed.

"You've changed clothes…but…how…"

Dread swept through her like a wildfire as she scrambled for words to explain.

Chapter Three

Paul squatted and reached to still Katy's hands when she began to tug on Fluffy's ears.

Fern stared at the top of his head, where his thick thatch of sandy hair shone like morning dew glistening in the first rays of the sun. What could she tell him? How could she explain? And why hadn't she anticipated Paul's curiosity over the clothes she'd conjured? Anxiety lay in her stomach like lead.

Stop being so hard on yourself, the voice whispered from the back of her brain. Why would she have imagined being questioned about her new wardrobe? No one in Sidhe would have thought a thing of her using magic to supply herself with something she needed. Where she came from everyone had some sort of magical ability. Granted, the power of some creatures was very weak, but whether it was controlling the weather or flying through the air or simply setting a cloud of dust into a whirl, no one she knew would have looked askance at using the gift of enchantment.

No one, that was, except Paul Roland. He wasn't from Sidhe and he didn't possess any magical powers.

When he tipped up his chin to look into Fern's face, his frown had disappeared and the corners of his mouth curled with what looked to be amazement.

"I can't believe the airline company delivered your bags already," he said. "That was fast. It's got to be a record."

Fern only blinked and kept quiet. If he was intent on answering his own question that was all the better for her.

"With the shape of the airline industry these days," Paul continued as he tugged Katy's sweater off, "I guess they're doing all they can to keep their customers happy."

Lifting one shoulder in a shrug, Fern softly said, "I guess."

"Well, I'm glad everything worked out and that you have your things. You must be pleased."

She thought of all the new garments she'd conjured while looking through the magazine this morning. She must have two dozen different outfits, all hanging neatly in the closet or folded in the drawers. A sheepish feeling sneaked over her as she thought she may have gone a bit overboard. "Very pleased, indeed," she told him.

"Wady!" Katy toddled over to Fern and reached to be picked up. Fern obliged. "Pway, wady."

"That's a grand idea," Fern said. "Let's go play. But first—" she tapped the child on her button nose

"—I want you to try to say my name. Say Fern for me."

Katy grinned. "Fun."

"That's it!" Fern laughed and smiled at Paul as she added, "Or close enough, anyway."

Paul chuckled. "It sure is strange how she's treating you like an old friend. She doesn't normally take to strangers."

"Oh, but we are old friends, aren't we, Katy?" Fern asked.

The toddler patted Fern's cheeks. "Fun."

"The two of you will be all right this morning while I work?" Paul asked.

Fern nodded. "Don't worry about us. We'll be just fine."

The morning flew by. Fern pulled out the blocks and stacked them in a tower again and again, while Katy waited patiently to knock them over. The stuffed bears on the shelf were perfect characters in the small play that Fern performed for the delighted toddler. And then the two of them took a walk out in the warm, late-morning sunshine. By noon Fern felt her stomach grumbling.

"I think it's time for some lunch, Katy-loo," she announced. Katy agreed by clapping her hands.

In the kitchen Fern searched for something to fix Katy for lunch. She found a loaf of bread. And she pulled open the ice box and saw a block of cheese. She turned her nose up at the beef she found in the drawer, the mere sight of it making her shiver.

Pulling open a cupboard, she grasped a jar of peanut butter. She knew what butter was, but had never heard of a peanut. She opened the lid and took a tentative sniff.

"Pea-budda!" Katy reached out with glee.

Fern dipped her finger into the soft, brown mass and took a taste. "Delicious," she said. Having seen humans make sandwiches oodles of times she smeared some peanut butter onto a slice of bread, folded it in half and gave it to Katy with a cup of milk.

By the time the child had finished eating, she was rubbing her eyes and getting cranky.

"Time for this little bairn to take a nap," Fern crooned as she wiped Katy's mouth and fingers with a damp cloth, then picked her up and took her upstairs to the nursery.

Settling herself into the white rocking chair, Fern sang an old Irish ditty as she swayed to and fro with Katy in her lap. Before long, the babe was sound asleep.

Fern tucked her in her crib, and then went down to clean up the mess she'd left in the kitchen. As Fern wiped up the last of the crumbs, her thoughts turned to Paul. She wondered how he was faring in his office.

It was then that she decided to make him a sandwich of peanut butter. Everyone had to eat, didn't they? And when she took him the food she prepared, she could see if he was making any headway on his new book. She poured him a tall glass of icy milk, placed it on the tray next to the sandwich, and then made her way through the house to his office.

She tapped on the door. "Hello?" she called, push-

ing open the six-paneled oak door with her elbow. "I
made you something to eat. Are you hungry?"

One look at his face told her that all was not well.

"What is it?" she asked.

Some low, ominous sound reverberated from deep
in Paul's chest. "Pardon my language, but I'm frustrated as hell," he grumbled. "I've been sitting here
for hours and I haven't written a single word."

Fern set the tray down on the edge of the desk.
"I'm sorry to hear that." The urge to reach out and
soothe the creases in his brow was overwhelming. To
resist the powerful impulse, Fern crossed her arms
over her chest.

"Where I'm from," she told him, "there's an
old—" she stopped short before using the word
gnome, doubting a gnome could be found in all of
America "—an old man who can tell wonderful stories. He doesn't write them down. Just tells them to
us from the front porch of the—of his home. I once
hung around after everyone else had gone. I asked
Alton where he came up with all those tales. He told
me that he often gets together with his friends, other
storytellers, and they swap ideas."

"Brainstorming is what we call that," Paul murmured.

"I like that word. A storm churning up the ideas
in the brain." She grinned. "That would surely get
the thoughts aflowin'. Maybe you should try it. Get
together with some of your friends. The people who
do the same thing you do. Swap some ideas. Stir up
a storm in your brain."

Fern was pleased when she saw her suggestion had
him smiling.

"That would be a good idea," he began, "but... you see, when Maire passed away, I kind of stepped away from the publishing world and all the people associated with it. My writing colleagues, too. I haven't kept in touch."

"Well, your friends, then. Call your friends. They'll talk to you about your problem. They might give you some ideas to get you started."

He was quiet a moment, then he confessed, "The truth is, I've been playing the turtle, Fern. I've tucked my head in...I've hunkered into my shell...I doubt my friends would want to hear from me after the way I cut myself off for so long."

It sounded like such an isolated existence. Fern tried one more time.

"Your family, then."

His small smile was sad. "I don't have much. No brothers or sisters. My dad passed away, I told you. I do see my mother a couple of times a year. She's retired to southern California. I call her often, of course, but—" he shook his head "—I don't want her to worry about me."

No colleagues. No friends. Very little family. Paul had no one he felt he could call on.

"How sad."

"Oh, now—" he waved away her concern "—don't feel bad for me. I do just fine. Katy is all I need. We have a great time together."

Then he picked up the sandwich she made him, almost getting it to his mouth before doing a double take.

"Peanut butter?" he asked.

She was surprised by his surprise. "Yes. Katy loves the stuff."

"And milk?"

"Milk is good for you," Fern told him. "It builds strong bones." Her affinity for human tots had her risking the scorn of her pixie friends. But during her close proximity Fern had overheard many parents using these very words when urging their children to drink their milk.

He chuckled. "I guess it does, at that." He raised one brow. "Did you see there was roast beef in the fridge?"

She shuddered. "I don't eat meat."

"Ah, so you're a vegetarian."

Fern nodded. "If that's what it's called, then that's what I am."

He took a bite, chewed and swallowed. "You didn't have to make lunch for me. I told you that. Your job is to watch Katy. You're not here to serve me."

She shrugged. "Everyone has to eat." Then she admitted, "Katy was napping, and I got to wonderin' how you were doin' in here. Bringing lunch was only an excuse to find out."

Paul put down the sandwich. "Well, as you can see, I'm not doing all that well." He reclined against the chair back and looked at the big, blank screen.

"I don't know how you do it," she said.

"Do what?"

"How do you go through life without anybody to talk to. To count on." Before he could answer, she continued, "Back in Sidhe, I have oodles of friends. We're together every single day. We laugh together.

If one of us gets the blues, the others are there to cheer her up. We get into all sorts of mischief together. I don't know what I'd do without them.''

She relaxed her hands at her sides. "You seem like the most alone person I've ever met.''

The room was terribly quiet.

Finally Paul said, "I'm not alone. I told you...I've got Katy.''

He knew immediately that he hadn't convinced her.

The sigh he heaved was huge. "Look, Fern, there are many different ways to handle grief. Some people reach out to others, lean on them heavily. Some people don't. I'm one of those who choose not to lean on others. I never want to be a burden on my friends...on my mother. I'm a strong person. I can handle my own problems.

"Granted," he continued, "for a while I was pretty angry at the world. But I'm over all that now.''

"If you're over all that, why are you still—'' the smile she offered him was very tiny "—playing the turtle?''

He couldn't help but grin as he lifted both hands, palms up. "Guess I just got used to the solitary life.''

Fern watched as he reached for the sandwich she'd made him. His strong jaw worked as he munched on it. The solitary life he described sounded so...lonely. Fern understood the vast amount of happiness and joy even one friend could bring into a person's life.

Well, Paul's isolated existence was just one more problem around here that needed fixing. And it would be fixed, too. At least, it would if she had any say in the matter.

* * *

Fern went into the house through the back door with Katy in tow. They'd spent the entire afternoon prowling around the paddocks and supply buildings on the property. A delicious smell permeated the air—tangy onions, sweet carrots and the fresh scent of celery urging Fern to inhale deeply.

When they entered the kitchen, she saw Paul standing at the stove, a white, bibbed apron covering his knit shirt and trousers.

"Ah—" he greeted them with a bright smile "—great timing. Dinner's nearly ready."

Fern was so pleased to see him in such good spirits.

"Something sure smells good," she told Paul. "But this little critter needs a quick washin' up first, I'm afraid. We found some nooks and crannies to explore today, and we got ourselves a wee bit grimy."

Hurrying Katy through the kitchen, Fern headed toward the stairs. Behind her, Paul called, "Don't be long."

"We won't," she assured him.

Upstairs she picked out a fresh outfit for Katy, and then made her way to the bathroom. She turned on the tap, stripped the toddler out of her dirty clothes and plopped her into the tub.

She scrubbed Katy from head to toe, pausing long enough in her swift movements to tickle her belly with the soapy washcloth.

"Let me get behind your ears," Fern said. Then she rinsed the soap from the cloth and used it to wipe away the sudsy residue on Katy's delicate skin.

"Clean as a whistle," Fern proclaimed. Then she pulled the child from the bath and enfolded her in a fluffy towel. "Are y' hungry?" she asked, slipping the pink T-shirt over Katy's head.

The toddler nodded vigorously.

She took a minute to wash her own face and hands, then they went back downstairs, following the spicy scent of whatever it was that Paul had fixed for them to eat.

"How's my little girl?" Paul planted a kiss on top of Katy's head.

When his lips made contact with the child's silken hair, Fern felt a strange heat spark inside her. It curled in a peculiar dance, and the amazing phenomenon set her to wondering. She sat down at the table with a mental shrug, blaming the odd feeling on the fact that she was famished.

"I made a vegetable stir-fry," Paul told her.

Fern wasn't really sure how to eat this stir-fry, but she watched and followed Paul's lead. He scooped out a small pile of white, fluffy bits. Rice, he called it. Then he ladled the steaming vegetables on top. A thick broth clung to them and dribbled down into the rice. It was the most luscious concoction that Fern had ever put in her mouth.

"This is *wonderful*," she told him, scooping up another bite onto her fork.

Katy picked up a soft, steamed carrot round with her fingers.

"Honey, use your spoon," Paul gently scolded his daughter.

Using meticulous care, the toddler placed the orange disk on her spoon and then guided it into her mouth. After chewing and swallowing, she licked the sauce from her fingertips.

The adults chuckled at her antics.

"So, was the afternoon any more productive for you?" Fern asked.

A gray cloud seemed to form over Paul as he shook his head.

"It's okay, though." He rubbed the pale-blue linen napkin between his thumb and index finger. "The muse will come when it's ready. It always does."

He was trying his darnedest to make her think he was okay with this problem of his, but Fern could tell he was feeling vexed about his inability to put the tale in his head down on paper. The powerful vibrations emanating off him told the true story of the frustration his benign expression was attempting to hide.

Her mind churned as she wondered how she might help him. Harping on it, she decided, was probably the last thing she should do. So she turned the discussion to other things.

"Katy and I found a small mountain of old tires out behind one of the barns."

"I've been meaning to have them carted away," Paul told her.

Fern grinned at the little girl. "We climbed them, didn't we, Katy-loo?"

Paul looked surprised. "But they must be filthy."

Chuckling, Fern said, "How do you think we got so dirty?"

"Those tires aren't safe for Katy to be playing on."

Anxious that he was doubting her ability to care for his daughter, Fern rushed to say, "We were very careful. I was right with her every second."

Katy's frustrated grunt had their gazes turning. The toddler was having an awful time trying to keep the slippery, sauce-coated rice on her spoon. Finally she pinched some of the gooey stuff in her fingers and carefully set it on her spoon before popping the food into her mouth. The glee on her face shouted *victory!*

Paul and Fern shared a smile, and the heat that had coiled in her tummy began snaking its way into her limbs.

"I'm sure you were careful," he assured her softly. "But maybe it's time I bought Katy a swing set. Or a jungle gym. Or a combination of both."

Fern had never heard of the things Paul mentioned, so she just remained quiet.

"What do you say, Katy? Should Daddy take you to the toy store tomorrow?"

Katy dropped her spoon and clapped. Rice, bits of vegetable and brown sauce went flying.

"Whoa, there!" Paul laughed. "You'll get all of us as messy as you, you little wench." He looked at Fern. "She's going to need another bath before she goes down for bed."

Fern smiled. "I don't mind. She loves a bath—"

"No, no," he told her. "If you don't mind, I'd like to spend some time with her. I'll clean her up, get her into her pj's and read her a book or two before putting her down for the night."

He slid his chair back and picked up his plate.

"Wait," Fern said. "I'll clean up here. You go have some fun with Katy."

Katy held fast to Paul's index finger. Watching father and daughter walk down the hallway, Fern felt her heart pinch with emotion so poignant it almost hurt.

* * *

Fern zipped through the air, flipping a joyous triple somersault as she entered Katy's room. She'd rushed to clean up the dinner mess as quickly as she could because she wanted to watch Paul interacting with Katy.

He was just getting her dressed after her second bath of the night, and from the looks of it, he got just about as wet in the process as she had.

Once Katy was all snapped up in her soft jersey pajamas, Paul settled her in her crib with several stuffed animals.

"Daddy needs to change his shirt," he told Katy. "You got me soaked."

Delight chimed in the toddler's giggle.

Fern hovered over the head of the crib. She'd keep Katy company until Paul returned.

He tugged his shirt over his head, and Fern was so overwhelmed by the awesome sight of his bare chest that her wings stopped beating. She plummeted through the air and came to a bouncy landing on the soft blanket bunched on the crib mattress. She fought her way out of the folds of fleecy fabric, her red curls hanging in her face. She pushed the locks out of her eyes just in time to see Paul striding toward the door.

Her eyes skittered over his broad shoulders, and she couldn't help but notice how his forearms were knotted with lean sinew. Corded muscle played just beneath his skin, and her gaze ate up the sight as it made its way down the long expanse of his back to his trim waist.

Paul disappeared through the doorway just as Katy's hand closed over Fern's body.

The toddler squealed with glee, and Fern's whole world went topsy-turvy.

"Le-go, Katy-loo!" Fern called. "Let me go!"

Katy's grip relaxed, and once again Fern was free-falling through the air. She got her wings fluttering just in time to avert disaster, then she spun around and soared up toward the ceiling. The child's laughter was joyous. Fern couldn't very well feel annoyed. Being captured in Katy's small fist had been Fern's own fault. She shouldn't have gotten so wrapped up in ogling Paul's bare torso.

Entertaining Katy was easy enough, and the flying maneuvers were actually quite fun after having been in that heavy human form all day.

Before too long Paul returned and plucked his daughter from the crib. Fern flew to the dresser and sat on the edge as Paul settled Katy onto the floor and sat down beside her. He reached for the shape-sorter toy and dumped out the brightly colored circles, triangles and squares. After naming each shape, he dropped it into its matching hole in the container and then urged Katy to do the same.

"I missed you today," he said. He smoothed his fingertips over Katy's milky cheek. "Did you have fun with Fern?"

"Fun!" Katy's head bobbed in answer.

"That's good. I think you like Fern, don't you?"

Again she nodded.

Fern's heart warmed at the exchange. Learning that Katy enjoyed being with her was gratifying.

"I like her, too," Paul said.

All of a sudden Fern felt breathless.

He smiled at his daughter. "And it sure doesn't hurt that she's so pretty to look at."

Katy tapped together a yellow circle and a blue triangle.

Paul gazed off toward the window, his voice lowering to a whisper as he said, "That riot of red curls. And I can't decide if those turquoise eyes of hers are more blue…or more green."

The emotion that sprouted to life in Fern was the most intense she'd ever experienced. Paul was thinking about her. Pondering her hair, her eyes. And if the tiny smile that played at the corners of his mouth was any indication, he was pleased with his thoughts.

Katy yawned, and Paul picked her up and tucked her into his lap as he sat down in the rocker.

"Let's look at a book before bed." He pulled the picture book of Maire's from the shelf and opened the cover. Katy gazed at the colorful pictures and then turned the pages as she was ready for a new one.

"Pwitty," she announced, pointing down at the page.

"The pixie is pretty," Paul agreed.

"Fun," Katy said. "Pwitty Fun."

Paul chuckled. "It does look a little like our Fern, doesn't it?"

Fern took to the air and hovered just over Paul's shoulder. Sure enough, the pixie that Maire had painted looked just like Fern. Just like the one Maire had painted of Fern on Katy's wall.

Fern landed on the high back of the rocking chair, balancing herself against its gentle swaying motion. Katy curled up in her father's lap, her head nestled against his chest. Paul kissed her on the temple.

Having rocked the toddler to sleep this afternoon, Fern remembered the wonderful tenderness that had coursed through her—a wonderful, almost achy feeling.

That must be what motherhood felt like.

Motherhood. As far as Fern knew, pixies didn't possess deep maternal feelings. Fern remembered her own parents. Her pixie mother, her brownie father. But like other woodland creatures, birds and foxes and bears, fairy parents raised their children, kept them fed and warm and safe, until that moment when they were old enough to fend for themselves. It's just the way of the world in Sidhe.

But Fern sure had fallen hard for Maire's little daughter. And it must have been her feelings for Katy that had enabled Fern to metamorphose into human form, or she supposed that was what had caused her to change so amazingly quickly in that airplane.

And Fern had always had intense feelings for human children. Wasn't she always getting into trouble for visiting nurseries and schoolyards? She'd loved Maire so when Maire had been an infant.

So it's quite possible that, for some odd reason, Fern possessed those mysterious, humanlike maternal instincts.

Suddenly she found herself wondering what it would be like to have a beautiful babe of her own. The miracle of human birth was something unknown to her. It had to be something similar to the animal babes she'd seen delivered in the forests of Sidhe. Fern knew enough to understand that it all began with a female...and a male. A woman and a man.

From her vantage point, she could only see one side

of Paul's face and the tip of his nose as he gazed down at his drowsy daughter. His eyelashes were several shades darker than his sandy hair, and she could see the beginnings of a tawny-shadowed beard darkening his jaw.

She contemplated what it might be like to have a child with this oh-so-handsome man. No sooner had the thought entered her head than Fern was besieged with a forceful sensation.

Oh, my! All these emotional thoughts were imposing a transformation. She was going to become human. Right here! Right now!

But…but she thought the rule was that no human eye could see—

Panic had her winging toward the doorway. She barely got around the corner and out into the hall when she changed into flesh and blood, skin and bone. Her heart was pounding like an army of trolls marching to war as she hurried into her bedroom and shut the door.

Her face was flushed, and she was quaking from head to foot. She'd thought that she couldn't change where anyone could see, but she was certain that, had she not zipped out of Katy's room the instant she had, Paul would have witnessed her transformation.

Were the rules altering themselves? Could such a thing happen?

She was going to have to be careful about her thoughts. Getting herself all worked up about Katy and motherhood and maternal instincts had been dangerous.

But wait. Her last thought hadn't been about Katy

at all. It hadn't been about motherhood, either. She went over those last few seconds in Katy's room.

Paul had been the seed planted in her fertile thoughts just before she'd nearly lost control. Fern sat down on the bed, her mind whirling. She tried to remember the times she'd metamorphosed.

"By me heart!" she whispered the oath aloud.

Could it be possible? She'd been thinking that Katy was the reason she had the ability to turn human. But it wasn't Katy at all.

She breathed in awe. "It's been Paul all along."

Chapter Four

Later that same evening, Fern left the close confines of her room still feeling confused about the revelation regarding her ability to transform. Realizing it was the man triggering the change, and not the child, totally bewildered Fern. What other aspects of her human transformation was she ignorant of? The question was both daunting and overwhelming.

"There you are."

The sound of Paul's soft voice shook her out of her reverie. Fern glanced up to see him standing at the base of the stairs. The mere sight of him had a smile canting one corner of her mouth.

"I thought your day with Katy may have tuckered you out and sent you to bed," he continued. "I am sorry that I didn't help you more today."

"Don't be silly." She descended the final step, the heated scent of him enveloping her like a warm, invasive mist. Fern kept her hold on the wide, oaken banister. "Watching little Katy is me job, right?"

Even though her tummy was tight with turmoil, she forced up a smile for him. A nice, bright one this time. He'd had a rough day, she knew, what with the frustration he'd had with his writing. He didn't need her anxieties adding to his troubles. Besides that, he would neither understand nor believe her anxieties. It was hard, at times, for *her* to believe this strange phenomenon that was happening to her.

The tension in his shoulders eased, and he returned her smile. "Would you join me for a glass of wine?" he asked.

She wasn't certain how wise it was to get any closer to Paul. Because he was the reason she was able to change from pixie to human, she'd have to be careful being around him in her fairy form. But she was flesh-and-blood human at the moment, so she didn't see any harm in accepting his offer.

"I'd like that," she told him.

They took their glasses out onto the rear patio to enjoy the summer evening. Stars glimmered in the inky sky overhead, and moonlight cast a luminous glow over rolling meadows spiked with aging fence posts.

"It's so peaceful," Fern breathed. The wine he'd served her tasted nectar-sweet, and her tongue fairly sang with each sip.

"I love the quiet." He frowned. "Usually. But right now I'm finding it a little unsettling. My thoughts are racing, yet I feel they're too jumbled to flow."

"You really did have a bad day, didn't you?"

"I guess it's to be expected." He combed his fingers through his sandy hair. "I haven't sat down to write anything for two years. Hopefully, I'm just experiencing a slow start.''

Fern shifted on the seat. ''You want to talk about it? Your story, I mean? I'm no writer, I'm not even a very good story teller, but it might help for you to talk—'' she grinned ''—and for me to listen.''

Uncertainty glittered in his dark eyes for a moment, and at first she thought he just might balk at her suggestion. It could be that he was protective of his idea. Or that he was unsure of his story.

But that couldn't be, could it? He'd said his books were popular. That they sold well. Best-sellers is what he'd called them.

Then he said, ''I want to write a story about a man who attempts to cheat death. His motivation, of course, is that he hadn't behaved well over the course of his life, and as a result he's afraid to die. I've got a great beginning. And I've come up with a wickedly twisted ending where he gets his just deserts.''

''Sounds gruesome,'' she whispered, honesty filling her tone.

''I hope so. That's what I'm shooting for, anyway.'' He chuckled. ''However, I am having a bit of a problem with that gap called the middle. I won't write a story if it looks like it will sag between beginning and end. I need to come up with some really grisly action.''

Crickets chirped, and somewhere in the woods, tree frogs croaked.

''Death is a grisly subject all by itself.'' Being a fairy, Fern hadn't spent much time contemplating anything that was unpleasant. Doing so just went against the lighthearted life that pixies lived.

"Well, I'm afraid I need a little more."

"You wouldn't need anythin' more if you'd ever seen the dullahan." She shivered at the mere mention of the name.

"The dullahan?"

He looked intrigued, and he must have picked up on the fear palpitating through her. Paul sat up straighter in the lounge chair. She nodded.

"Big of stature—" she felt her eyes go wide "—and broad of shoulder, the dullahan is a fearsome creature. He rides the countryside on a swift black steed that breathes flames from its nostrils and sends thunder rolling across the valleys with its gargantuan hooves."

Nerves made her lips dry, and she paused long enough to moisten them with a swipe of her tongue.

"The dullahan covers his grotesque body with a long, black cloak," she continued. "And he carries his head, ya see. His fingers clutch his hair and he lifts his head up high. Otherwise, he can't see where he is goin'. The skin of his face is marred, like mouldy cheese. And it glows with some strange phosphorescence. It's eerie, and it's the scariest thing I've ever laid me eyes on."

Completely caught up in her experience now, she hadn't even realized the words she'd used. She pressed on. "His grin is diabolical. He looks insane, he does. But he's not, and don't let anyone tell you he is. He's got black beady eyes that can see into the future. He knows your fate, you see. Wherever the dullahan stops, a mortal dies. If he's about, you'd best close your eyes tight. He can make you go blind. And you should clap your hands over your ears, lest you hear him call your name. But there's no stopping yer bad fortune once the dullahan has pronounced your death fate.''

Her words held Paul rapt. His voice was whispery as he asked, ''So this dullahan is like the angel of death?''

''By me heart,'' Fern swore, shaking her head with such a jerk that a red curl fell across her face, ''he's no angel. Believe you me. He's a hideous creature, he is.'' She swiped the curly tress aside. ''And the scariest thing is, there's no stoppin' him. Gates and doors fly open to 'im, no matter how securely they're locked. No mortal is safe from the dullahan's cruel prophecy.''

''You said you'd seen him,'' Paul said, ''yet your sight is fine. How can that be?''

''Oh, our gazes didn't meet. When I saw the dullahan he was far up on the ridge.'' She held her wineglass in a death grip. ''I clapped me hands over me ears and squeezed me eyes shut tight. I heard a muffled groan and knew the dullahan had called out the name of some poor soul.'' Fern shivered. ''Less than an hour later, there was an accident on the ridge. Ian McCarthy was ridin' his mule home. The animal slipped on some shale stones, and Ian broke his neck in the fall. Poor fella. It was Ian's name the dullahan had called out, that's fer sure.''

Fern hadn't realized just how worked up she'd gotten. Her heart was racing, and a thin film of perspiration prickled the back of her neck. She took a deep breath and remembered that she wasn't in Sidhe. She was safe from the dullahan.

Paul's sudden merry laughter took her completely off guard. Her gaze flew to his face.

"I thought you said you couldn't tell a good story," he said, delight lighting in his mahogany eyes. "You were fabulous! I was riveted. That's just the kind of magic I try to conjure when I write. You were wonderful, Fern. You really know your Irish folklore, don't you?"

Oh, she was such an eejit! Of course, the dullahan would be folklore to him. He was a mortal.

Relating her encounter with Sidhe's hideous creature of death had set her insides to quivering. She shoved the trepidation aside and plastered a grin on her mouth. "Well, I guess being an average Irish lass means I can tell a tale better than some."

"Better than some?" Paul's dark brows arched a fraction. "I'd say better than most. You were quite entertaining, Fern."

"Well, thanks." Her head tilted to one side. "I'm glad I could make y' laugh. You're much too tense."

He nodded, his tawny hair slipping down onto his forehead. Fern had to use every ounce of her strength not to reach up and brush it back into place.

"I agree," he told her. "I have been too stressed...for too long."

She brightened when an enchanting idea popped into her head. "I know what we should do." She set her glass down on the side table. "Take off your shoes." Toeing her own sandals off, she waved for him to follow suit. "Come on, now. Trust me. Off with your shoes."

He slid his tanned feet out of the casual boat shoes he wore.

Fern stood, picked up her wine and then reached for Paul's hand. "There's nothing more relaxing than a barefoot stroll through the cool, evening grass."

He didn't look convinced, but he took her hand and let her lead him down the three small steps that led out into the backyard.

The grass was cool against her skin, the soft blades tickling her feet like feathers.

"It does feel nice," he finally agreed. He stopped in the middle of the yard, gulped down the last of his wine and then stared up at the stars. "Gee, it's beautiful, isn't it?"

"Yes." She scanned the dome of darkness from one side of the horizon to the other. "I love the way the pinpoints of light twinkle and flash. It's almost as if they're puttin' on a show just for me."

She stole a quick glance over at Paul, his profile lifted heavenward. He had a strong jaw. A nice, straight nose. And she liked the little hollow indentation just below each cheekbone.

"I can't tell you when I last took the time to just stand and study the sky." He looked over at her. "Or sit on the deck and enjoy the night. Or feel the grass between my toes. Lord, I'm pathetic."

"You're no such thing." Her tone held a mild warning. She didn't like hearing him talk about himself like that. "You're a single dad. You've been raising Katy all alone. I don't have any bairns of my own, of course, but it's hard enough with two people, I'm sure. You need to give yourself more credit. It's clear how much time and effort you put into being Katy's father. She's healthy and happy, and no one could want anything more than that now, could they?"

The whole time she argued in his favor, she felt some energy begin to spin and dance around her. Around them both. A force of some sort that had sent out potent fingers to entwine and entangle them.

Fern felt drawn to Paul, inch by excruciating inch. His handsome face grew taut, and she knew he was keenly aware of the strange power encircling them. He let go of her hand, reached up and touched the curls that were tucked close to her ear. His fingertips grazed her jaw, and she closed her eyes, leaning toward his touch.

The rich timbre of his voice whispering her name caused her heart to pound, her blood to throb. What was this marvelous feeling pumping through her being? she wondered. As a pixie, she'd never felt its like.

It was yearning.

But for what?

She felt in need of…something.

"Look at me." His order was gruffer now, and when she opened her eyes, she saw that he was experiencing that same raw…what?

"What is this?" she asked him, the husky words snagging in her throat. "I've never encountered anything like this in me life."

He traced her jaw, the outer rim of her ear, and Fern felt an amazing heat spark inside her. Warm tendrils curled, and the hunger burning deep in her belly grew more intense.

"You're innocent, Fern."

His tone grated harshly, and she got the distinct impression that he was becoming regretful about something. She just wished she knew what.

"You're too innocent for the likes of me."

Paul made to move away from her, but she reacted quickly, capturing his fingers between her palm and her cheek.

"You may see me as wide-eyed and ignorant," she said, "but I don't want to be either of those things. I don't know what this is, Paul. But I'd like you to teach me. Show me. I don't want to be an innocent."

He stared down into her face. "You know what's happening here. You're a grown woman. You know the things that go on between adults."

She remained silent. Finally his eyes widened.

"You're a virgin."

If that's what they called a grown human woman who had never experienced these feelings before, then Fern guessed that's what she was. She supposed she would eventually have felt this type of wondrous yearning, but probably not to this extent. Fern had learned that human emotion was much more intense than what she'd ever experienced as a fairy.

Pixies often did pair off with a male brownie—her own parents had—but not until they were old enough and wise enough to make such a complicated relationship work. Up until now, Fern had been having too much fun flitting and frolicking with her friends to even think about such a union. She hadn't fancied herself old enough or wise enough to go searching the forests for a brownie mate.

But the delicious feelings churning in her had stirred her curiosity. If bonding with a male meant she'd experience and explore these awesome feelings, then she was all for it.

However, she had to admit that she didn't like the

inflection in Paul's voice when he'd called her a virgin. He'd made it sound like a bad thing.

"Oh, Fern." He pulled his hand away. "This isn't right. I can't do this."

"Of course you can," she pleaded.

"No—" his tone was almost angry now "—I can't."

Confusion ripped through her. "But why not? I want to learn. I want to know. Show me, Paul."

"I'm not going to show you anything, Fern."

He turned on his heel and stalked toward the house, leaving her out in the middle of the yard trying to figure out the desperate and hungry sensations pumping through her body.

Fern awoke the next morning feeling tired. She hadn't slept well at all. Since arriving at Paul's house in America, she had spent her days as a mortal woman, and once Katy was fast asleep in her crib, Fern would transform back into a pixie. She'd fly cross the meadows and over the treetops, letting the wind whip through her curls. By the time she flew back into the bedroom window at night, she'd be exhilarated but exhausted. She would curl up on the pillow and let her eyelids close in sweet sleep. Every morning she'd awaken feeling refreshed and ready for a new adventure, and she'd change back into human form.

However, last night she'd been so discombobulated. The touch of Paul's fingertips against her cheek had ignited a fire in her. He'd touched off a hunger of some sort. She'd felt...starved. But it wasn't food she craved. What had been so confusing was that she wasn't sure what it was she needed to satiate this peculiar and all-consuming appetite that plagued her.

All she did know was that—whatever it was she yearned for—Paul was the key to it all. The intensity in his deep-brown eyes had made her weak in the knees. Feeling his skin on hers, she'd gotten the impression that he was stoking a fire. A blaze that was contained inside her.

It made no sense to her. But last night, she could tell that it *had* made sense to Paul. He understood the turmoil she was experiencing, even though she hadn't a clue what it was all about. He knew the secret. And when she'd pleaded with him to tell her, to show her, he'd refused. He'd actually seemed to have gotten angry before going into the house.

By the time she'd gathered her wits about her and gone inside, too, she'd discovered that Paul had locked himself away in his study. So she'd trudged up the steps and had lain on the mattress pondering it all.

Why wouldn't he reveal the secret? she wondered. Why wouldn't he satisfy the awesome and mysterious need that had seemed to devour her from the inside out?

He'd called her innocent. A virgin, he'd said. And the way he'd said it! As if it was some disease, something he was afraid to touch. She'd never heard the term before, but she was smart enough to figure out that a virgin was someone who wasn't privy to the secret Paul knew.

Well, she didn't want to be a virgin. And she wouldn't be for much longer if she could convince Paul to explain the wonderful mystery.

That the mystery was wonderful, she had no doubt. She'd tingled inside when she'd been out in the yard with Paul last night. And the heat…why, it had been amazing. Quenching that overwhelming thirst…that deep-seated hunger would be…well, it would be—

The words to describe what she was imagining eluded her.

In frustration she tossed back the thin cotton blanket and got out of bed. She looked down the length of her legs. By me word, she silently mouthed. She'd awakened in her human form! Or had she turned human while lying there thinking about Paul? She had no way of knowing, really.

She wiggled her bare toes. It felt strange to wake up and greet the morning without wings, without lifting herself into the air and taking flight in the glorious summer sunshine.

She looked outside and realized it was early. She had time for a quick buzz around the yard before Katy would awaken. She cranked open the window just a bit. Closing her eyes and crossing her hands over her chest, Fern smiled at the thought of winging through the air.

But then she blinked, her mouth flattening. Where were her wings? Why hadn't she changed?

A frown bit into her brow.

She'd quickly learned that the miracle of transforming did have its rules that needed to be followed. On the airplane she'd come to understand that no human eye could witness the change. But then she'd experienced that incident where she'd been sure she would have changed right in front of Paul and Katy had she not zoomed out of the nursery.

Fern sighed, wondering what could be keeping her mortally bound.

Movement in the periphery of her vision made her jump.

"Fluffy!" She reached for the fat cat, stroked his soft fur and picked him up. "How did you get in here?"

Fern nuzzled her cheek against Fluffy's velvety coat.

Could it be that no living being could witness the metamorphosis? Cats included? Still contemplating the question, she padded to the door, opened it and scooted Fluffy out into the hallway. He meowed his displeasure at being banished from the room, and Fern's lips twisted.

"Sorry," she whispered before quietly shutting the door.

Leaning her head against the locked bedroom door, Fern closed her eyes and crossed her hands over her chest. Her breathing became slow and rhythmic, and after several seconds had passed, she began to worry that she'd lost her ability to become a pixie.

Focus, she silently commanded herself. *Focus!*

She thought of Sidhe. Of her fairy friends. Of the elves and gnomes. Of the silkies swimming just offshore in the mist covered seas. Of her fellow pixies.

Fern felt herself growing lighter. Her wings sprouted and automatically began their rapid beating, and she was airborne in an instant. She zipped around the room, delight puttering through her veins, and then she slipped out the open window.

Summer aromas bombarded her senses—the wildflowers and fresh grass, the piney evergreens and the musky scent of a raccoon snoozing in the underbrush nearby.

Nothing set her heart to fluttering like flying. Absolutely nothing.

The thought had barely entered her head when she realized that it wasn't the truth. Paul's handsome face flashed in her brain. That intense gaze of his never failed to set her pulse pounding. The touch of his fingers made her positively weak. Paul sparked in her an exhilaration that couldn't be matched by anything.

One moment Fern was speeding along, the next she went sliding across the damp grass, her human arms and legs flailing. Nothing was hurt except her dignity, but the shorts she wore—which had surprisingly transformed along with her—sported a long, green stain on the hip.

She stood up and dusted herself off, shocked that she'd changed into a human at such an inopportune time. Had she been flying any higher, she'd have broken a bone or two. It seemed her control over this transformation business was becoming more and more erratic.

Her gaze swung toward the house. She looked up at her bedroom window on the second floor, and after only a moment of silent deliberation, she decided it would probably be safer to just walk back across the yard and go into the house through the back door.

The steps of the deck were rough under her bare feet. She reached for the handle on the door. It didn't budge. She was locked out.

It looked as though she was going to have to concentrate very hard so she could fly back in through her bedroom window. And she'd better hurry, too.

Katy would be waking soon. Fern closed her eyes, and after several futile moments, she was filled with frustration.

An exhalation left her in a rush, then she opened her eyes—

And saw that Paul was standing on the other side of the glass door staring at her. Well, no wonder she hadn't been able to get her wings to bud.

Sudden anxiety gnawed at her. Surely he would ask what she was doing outside. How was she going to explain?

She heard the latch on the door click and he opened it.

"You go for a walk and get locked out?" he asked.

Well, she had walked back to the house…and she was locked out. She nodded in answer.

Then she noticed that he looked tired. But his gorgeous brown eyes were dancing with some mysterious joy.

"What is it?" She paused, then added, "You look…strange."

He laughed, stepping back so she could enter.

"Not strange, exactly," she quickly amended. "You seem exhausted, but you also seem elated."

"I am," he said. "I'm both."

Although he was clearly fatigued, he fairly glowed with some vibrant energy.

"I didn't sleep," he told her. "I was up all night."

"Oh, by me heart," she swore softly. "I'm sorry, Paul. If there's something I can do—"

"No, no," he cut her off. "It's a good thing. I was writing. All night long. And it was all because of you."

Gratitude hummed from him like musical notes, and she basked in it.

"Your tale about the headless horseman—"

"The dullahan," she murmured, stifling a shudder as they made their way into the kitchen.

"Yes." He nodded. "Your description was delightfully eerie. It raised the hair on the back of my neck. And it heated up my imagination until it was boiling like a witch's cauldron."

He'd conjured a heat in her last night, too, she remembered. But she suspected that the two of them had gone through different experiences entirely. No, that wasn't entirely true. The same kind of mystical intensity that had plagued her had sparked a fire in him, too. Even if for only a moment. She'd witnessed it. Otherwise, she'd never have realized he was privy to the secret that she so desperately wanted.

His excitement about this unexpected burst of creativity was almost palpable, and Fern couldn't help but get caught up in it.

"That's wonderful, Paul."

He took down two glasses from the cabinet. "Juice?"

She nodded, then watched him open the refrigerator and retrieve the carton.

He continued to talk while he poured. "I decided to make my protagonist a bit older. He visits Ireland and encounters the dullahan."

It was impossible not to be captivated by his mood.

"The man is determined to cheat death."

"Oh," Fern breathed, "it's impossible to escape the dullahan."

Paul's head bobbed. "I intend to show that. It will

seem as if the man succeeds in his plans. It will look as if he's completely duped the dullahan. But then comes the twist.''

His laughter was dark, and it caused a shiver to course across her skin.

''My protagonist has an accident,'' Paul told her. ''Ends up in a convalescent facility for physical therapy...and is murdered by a nursing assistant working there. At the last instant before losing consciousness, the killer whispers the man's name, then offers up a diabolical grin. The reader will know the nursing assistant isn't a nursing assistant at all.''

Fern felt her eyes go wide. ''It's the dullahan.''

''Exactly.''

''Paul, that's frightening.''

He grinned. ''It is, isn't it? My editor is going to like it. Better yet, my readers are going to love it. I can just feel it. Oh, and I managed to come up with several really great twists in the plot that will avoid a boring and saggy middle.''

''That's wonderful.''

He turned from the counter, his gaze riveted to her face. ''It's because of you. Because of your story and the emotion you used when you told it. I feel as if you broke through the barrier, Fern. I don't know how to thank you.''

Her heart pinched behind her ribs. ''You just did.'' She smiled. ''I'm glad I could help you.''

Helping him made her feel as if she could soar through the air, even without her pixie wings.

Paul handed her the orange juice, looking troubled suddenly. ''I'm sorry about the way we parted last night,'' he told her. ''We need to talk about that.''

"Yes," she agreed emphatically. They did need to talk about what had happened between them. He had the secret. And she wanted it. She was determined to get it.

Just then Katy cried out, and both of them turned their heads instinctively toward the stairs leading to the child's room.

"I'll go get her," Fern offered. She speared him with a narrow gaze. "But we will talk later, right?"

"Yes," he assured her, "we will talk later."

Chapter Five

Paul awoke with a start. Just before lunch, he'd lain down on the couch in his study with the intention of resting his eyes. The numbers on the clock now read 7:52 p.m. The last vestiges of daylight glowed orange through the window. He'd slept away the entire afternoon. He sat up, and seeing the cotton throw that covered him, he smiled. Looked as though Fern had taken care of him, yet again.

An image of Fern's sexy blue-green eyes floated in his mind. Her delicate, creamy complexion. Her mop of burnished curls. His breath hitched in his dry throat as desire quickened his body.

He wanted her, that much he knew. And he'd toyed with the idea of having her, too. But after finding out last night just how innocent she was...

A virgin! He had no right to play around with something so dangerous.

Kissing her, touching her, tasting her—the urges

were becoming more and more insistent. But she was pure and naive. She wouldn't be able to handle the powerful emotions that accompanied casual teasing and flirtation. He vividly sensed that much. He saw it in the exuberant way she reacted to everyday happenings. Her inexperience had kept her from honing the skill necessary to keep her feelings in check.

She was in the States all on her own, far away from her family and friends. Fern would have nowhere to go, no one to turn to, if she were to lose control, if she were to get hurt while the two of them experimented with passion.

His protective instinct had been triggered from the very first time he'd met her on that airplane. Harming her in any way was the last thing he wanted to do.

But her lips had looked so inviting, and her heavy-lidded eyes had seemed to call out to him.

I want to learn. I want to know. Show me...

Her plea haunted him, and he felt his body grow rigid in response.

Just then the door of his study creaked open, and Katy gasped with glee. "Daddy!"

"We came to see if you were awake," Fern said, pushing the door open wide. "Katy's ready for bed and she wanted to kiss you good-night."

His daughter toddled toward him, and he scooped her up onto his lap. Her hair was silky and slightly damp, and her skin smelled of baby soap.

"You've had a bath." The sloppy kiss he planted on her cheek elicited a giggle from her. "You smell so good, I could eat you up!" He nuzzled her neck and she wiggled in his arms, obviously tickled to have his attention. "Did you have fun with Fern today?"

"Fun!" Katy squealed.

Paul looked at Fern. "I'm sorry I fell asleep."

"Ach—"

He loved the velvety burr in her voice.

"You're bein' silly," she told him softly. "You needed your rest."

"Well, that much is true." He set Katy down and ran his fingers through his hair. "How about if I come up with you to put her to bed?" He ruffled Katy's hair. "Would you like for Daddy to read a story to you?"

"Sto-wee!" Katy clapped with enthusiasm.

The three of them trudged up the stairs, and Paul let Katy choose a book. She wasn't happy having just one story read to her, so he indulged her with a second. By the time he'd closed the book, she was rubbing her eyes and yawning.

Fern plucked the toddler from his lap and cradled Katy in her arms. "You need to go to bed, sweet pea," Fern crooned.

He got up and whispered, "I'm going to have a shower."

Fern nailed him with a firm gaze. "We can meet downstairs when you're finished?" she asked, evidently fearful that he'd forgotten. "So we can talk?"

He nodded, kissed his sweet Katy on the forehead and then headed for the door.

Not too much later he descended the steps feeling rejuvenated. Nothing was as reviving on a warm evening as a cool shower. He'd shaved and changed into clean clothes, but even the extra energy the long nap had provided couldn't take away the unease he felt regarding the talk Fern seemed determined to have. But he'd promised, so he intended to see it through.

He found her sitting at the kitchen table, her fingers curled around a tall glass of iced tea.

"Would you like something to drink?" she asked the instant he came into the room.

"Sit still," he told her. "I'll get it." He pulled a tumbler from the cabinet and poured himself some tea. Ice cubes plunked from the pitcher into the glass.

In an effort to put off the intimate conversation he knew was to come, he said, "I want to thank you again for explaining that Irish folktale. I can't explain how that fable opened the door of my imagination. I was wondering…"

He was very aware of how her fingers slid down the condensation that had collected on the outside of her glass.

She asked, "What were you wondering?"

"If you could tell me more," he said. "Not now. I'm not ready yet. I'm still plotting out the skeleton of my story. But later…I'll need other characters, other mythical creatures to help flesh out the imaginary world I'm creating. Could you give me more information?"

"Of course. There are plenty of fairy creatures lurking about. More than would ever fit in a book, I'm sure." She grinned. "Gully dwarves and gnomes, cluricauns and changlings. Leprechauns. Brownies. Silkies. Imps. Elves." Her voice became soft as she added, "And pixies. We can't forget the pixies. I'll be happy to tell you about them all—"

Her chin dipped demurely, and Paul was struck with the notion that it was just about the most alluring sight he'd ever beheld. He wanted to curl his fingers under her jaw, tip her face upward, kiss her soft and tempting lips.

"—if it would help your writing."

"It would, Fern," he told her honestly, doing everything he could to push the improper thoughts from his head. "It truly would."

Her blue-green gaze went serious. "I'm willin' to give y' what y' want," she said. "Will y' give me what I'm lookin' for? I want the secret, Paul. Tell me all you know."

He averted his face from hers a fraction, a silent but clear denial.

"You made me feel things," she pressed. "Mysterious things I've never felt before in me whole entire life. Something—" she pressed her palm against her solar plexus "—deep inside. An…unanswered call. A…a hunger that has nothing to do with food. Some kind of—" The rest of her thought went unspoken as obvious frustration had her expression screwing up. She shook her head, her curls bouncing. "I can't adequately explain it."

He chuckled. "Great minds have tried to do just that and have failed." When she remained silent and staring, he frowned. "You're serious. Fern, didn't your parents explain any of this to you? I'd think they would, knowing the state of the world."

"It's hard to imagine, but the place I come from is far away from the world you live in." Her chin dipped as she admitted. "Such things aren't talked about."

Her innocence was sweet…and perilously alluring.

A case of nerves had him clearing his throat. "I'm

not sure how to go about this,'' he began. ''Through the ages, people have tried to find the words to truly capture the essence of all those things you're feeling. They've failed, one and all.'' He rested an elbow on the tabletop. ''Describing the overwhelming emotions involved with...desire—'' there, he thought, he'd put a name to what they were discussing ''—is futile because no one has ever been able to explain the enigma of it. The miracle of it.'' He paused long enough to take a deep breath. ''And I believe no one ever will. It's a beautiful thing that eludes description.''

Her face went serious. ''Then if you can't tell me...I'd like you to show me.''

Paul frowned, worrying his bottom lip between his teeth while he carefully planned and measured his words. ''Honey,'' he began haltingly, ''you don't know what you're asking.''

He was bombarded by her myriad emotions—confusion, angst, eagerness, anxiety. Even though he knew it was probably a mistake, he reached over and slid his palm over her hand. Her skin felt warm and soft against his. And he did his best to ignore the current that hummed between them.

''I'm going to attempt to explain this, okay?'' he said. ''But you're going to have to be patient with me.''

She nodded.

''Attraction. Desire. Passion. All of the things relating to...intimacy between a man and a woman...'' His voice petered out as he strove to find the right words. ''Intimacy. Communion—'' his breath skipped, but he forced out ''—sex.'' He exhaled, realizing that this was even more difficult than he'd imagined it would be. "The act of sex can be a wonderful thing or...or a not-so-wonderful thing."

Fern's brow was puckered. She was trying to understand, but he knew he wasn't going about this very clearly.

"You see," he continued, "sex—the physical act of...of joining—shouldn't be enacted unless the people involved have a chance to, well, to fall in love. Otherwise sex becomes lust. And lust, although it might feel good for a few moments, leaves a person feeling empty inside. Unfulfilled. Hollow and pointless."

The room seemed too quiet.

"What you're tellin' me is—" her voice was a mere whisper "—that you need to fall in love with me before you can show me the sex that will make me feel fulfilled."

Oh, Lord, he thought. What the hell have I done?

"That's not quite what I'm saying," he rushed to say. "Fern, not every man and woman who meet feel the kind of attraction that leads to love."

Bewilderment clouded her gaze. "So you aren't attracted to me?"

He'd be lying if he gave her an affirmative answer.

"But," she continued, her voice growing stronger as she leaned forward, "I know you felt the same thing I felt. I saw it in your eyes. I felt it swimmin' around the two of us. You can't tell me you didn't feel it."

Paul let his eyelids fall shut for a moment. He felt as if he were digging a hole for himself, and no amount of talk was going to get him out of it.

He looked at her. "You're right. I can't tell you I didn't feel it."

She nodded. Was that smugness he saw curling the corner of her luscious mouth?

"However, just because we're attracted to each other—" he curled his hand into a fist and set it in his lap "—doesn't mean it will lead to the kind of relationship needed in order for us to...to..."

"Have meaningful sex," she finished for him.

"Exactly."

She sat silent for a moment, and he could see questions churning in her head. For some reason, he got the distinct feeling that he should run away. Fast.

Her eyebrows bobbed as an idea evidently struck her.

"What if I'm willing to have some meaningless sex?" she asked bluntly.

Paul thought he'd have a heart attack right there. "Y-you don't m-mean that," he sputtered. "You aren't willing to do that. You wouldn't put yourself in that position." He garnered his wits quickly. "And even if you would, I wouldn't. So forget that idea altogether."

"Oh," she said. "Okay. I just thought I'd ask." Then her forehead pinched again. "If y' don't mind me asking, why won't y' have some meaningless sex with me?"

He was hit with a fresh bout of palpitations. Lifting his hand, he scrubbed at his jaw with agitated fingers.

"What you need to understand—" he lowered his voice as he added "—what I'm obviously not explaining clearly enough, is that making love is a miracle. It's something special that should take place between a man and a woman who have deep feelings for each other. And that's especially so in your case.''

"In my case? Why is my case special?''

"Because it will be—'' why were the words sticking in his throat? ''—your first time.''

Out of the blue she said, "Tell me about your first time, then.''

"You don't want to hear—''

"I do,'' she insisted.

"You don't. I was a young and randy teenager bent on losing my virginity with the first person I could find.''

Her eyes widened. "That's exactly how I'm feelin'!''

Laughter ripped from his throat before he could stop it. "You are not, Fern. That's not what you're feeling at all. What you're feeling is curiosity. And that's a natural human instinct.''

"And being randy isn't natural?''

He chuckled. "When I was a teenager it probably was. But we're not teenagers. And you do want to respect yourself. You deserve to be respected by others.''

She folded her hands and placed them on the table in front of her. "If that's what meaningful sex is about, then I guess you're right.''

"Good,'' he said. "I'm glad we got that much cleared up, at least.'' He lifted his glass of tea and took a swallow.

"Would you tell me about the first time you had meaningful sex?''

The glass he held hit the table with a thump. He

was so relieved that he'd already swallowed the mouthful of tea. He'd have spewed it everywhere.

She added, "I'd guess that your first time would have been with Maire."

Memories walloped him from all sides. Maire's dark eyes loomed in his mind. "Yes." His throat was too tight to say more than that.

When his wife had died, Paul had believed there would never be another woman that would affect him as his Maire had done. But he realized that the attraction he felt for Fern was just as powerful.

She reached over and touched his forearm. "Don't be sad, Paul."

He blinked. Evidently, she'd taken his silence as grief.

"You want to talk about it?" she offered.

Heat rushed to his face. "My relationship with Maire is...too private for me to talk about comfortably."

What he was really feeling was a tad embarrassed. He'd been thinking of Maire, yes. But Fern had been in his thoughts, as well.

Those blue-green eyes of hers turned troubled suddenly.

"What's bothering you, Fern?"

She looked away and then leveled her gaze on him. "I have a question. But I don't know if I should ask. It may be too personal."

"Of course you should ask. If you go too far, I'll let you know." He gave her a small smile of encouragement.

"Your relationship with Maire...it was close."

She didn't pose her words as a question, but he could tell she wanted some response from him.

"Yes," he obliged. "Maire and I were very much in love."

"Well," she began tentatively, "now that she's... gone...does that mean you can't ever have fulfilling sex with anyone else ever again?"

The silence was thick and heavy. He had no idea what to say.

He thought at first that if he remained silent she might tiptoe away from the topic, but she never faltered. Her gaze held his steadily, and it was clear to him that she was determined to have an answer of some sort.

"I really don't know, Fern," he finally told her. "But if this is about me and you, if you're asking me if we can engage in meaning—"

"No." She shook her head. "It isn't about me. This is about you. I'm worried."

Uncertain of where she was going with the conversation, he went quiet and waited.

"Those feelings that you conjured in me," she slowly continued. "That attraction. That...needy heat. It was amazing. And if Maire was the only person who would allow you to feel those things, and she's no longer around, I think it would be very sad if you...you know, could never experience the miracle of meaningful sex again."

He lifted his hand, rested his thumb near his chin. Nervously he traced a short line back and forth across his jaw with his curled index finger. Her concern for him was touching. Heady emotion roiled in his chest, making him feel as if a steel band was being tightened around his torso.

"I don't think Maire would want you to be alone," Fern said. "Just think about it, Paul. If circumstances had been different, if Maire had been the one who was left all alone with wee Katy, would you want her to be on her own? Would you want her to never feel loved again?"

Paul searched Fern's face and could find not a single nuance of selfish intent there. Her eyes were clear and filled with nothing but sincere concern for him.

He couldn't help but take note that she'd wanted to talk to him about sex. He had known she'd wanted him to show her what making love was all about. However, the moment he'd shown the smallest trace of what she'd interpreted as sorrow, she'd forgotten all about herself and put every thought and word into consoling him. Into solving his problems. It's what she had done from the very first moment they had met—focused on him and the solving of his troubles.

She was one amazing woman, he realized. And the things she'd pointed out made his thoughts spin.

New York City was a place like no other, Fern decided as she walked along the sidewalk next to Paul, drinking in all the sights and sounds. Shops of every description flanked streets that teemed with people, young, old and every age in between. Every pedestrian seemed in an awful rush.

The aromas were amazing. They passed one doorway, and the rich scent of baking bread wafted around them. Just a few steps farther down the block, an unusual but rich spicy fragrance assaulted her nostrils.

Then they passed a street vendor, and Fern's mouth salivated when she smelled the sharp tang of mustard.

It had been more than a week since Fern and Paul had had their intense discussion about love and lust and the differences in the physical relationships involved with each. Paul had identified for her the vibrations that hummed between them, calling them attraction. And although he'd made it plain that he had no intention of showing her what sex was all about, that hadn't stopped the unseen current that swirled and skipped around them whenever they were together.

The fact that she'd never experienced sex before seemed to play an important part in Paul's not wanting to reveal the secret to her. She guessed she could approach another human man about having sex, but instinct told her that no one else but Paul could conjure those amazing feelings in her.

So what was it she was feeling for him? Lust? Or love?

She knew that love brought along with it sex that meant something between the two partners. Lust brought sex that didn't. Paul had made that clear enough. But other than that, she didn't know much about the differences between love and lust. She'd wanted to ask Paul about the matter, but he'd been so busy with his writing.

He had worked feverishly on his book for days, keeping himself sequestered for long hours at a stretch. However, this morning he'd announced that he wanted to take Fern and Katy into the city for the day. Excitement made Fern's heart race, and she was

NO POSTAGE
NECESSARY
IF MAILED
IN THE
UNITED STATES

BUSINESS REPLY MAIL

FIRST-CLASS MAIL   PERMIT NO. 717-003   BUFFALO, NY

POSTAGE WILL BE PAID BY ADDRESSEE

SILHOUETTE READER SERVICE
3010 WALDEN AVE
PO BOX 1867
BUFFALO NY 14240-9952

Play the Lucky Hearts Game

and get...

2 FREE BOOKS
and a FREE MYSTERY GIFT...

yes!
YOURS to KEEP!

I have scratched off the silver card. Please send me my **2 FREE BOOKS** and **FREE mystery GIFT.** I understand that I am under no obligation to purchase any books as explained on the back of this card.

Scratch Here!

then look below to see what your cards get you... 2 Free Books & a Free Mystery Gift!

309 SDL DZ5R

209 SDL DZ56

FIRST NAME	LAST NAME

ADDRESS

APT.#	CITY

STATE/PROV.	ZIP/POSTAL CODE

(S-R-06/04)

Twenty-one gets you
2 FREE BOOKS
and a **FREE MYSTERY GIFT!**

Twenty gets you
2 FREE BOOKS!

Nineteen gets you
1 FREE BOOK!

TRY AGAIN!

Offer limited to one per household and not valid to current Silhouette Romance® subscribers. All orders subject to approval.

enjoying being with Paul, being with Katy, exploring the bustling streets.

Window after window displayed colorful merchandise for sale. Dresses and shoes, scarves and handbags. Jewelry that glinted in the sunlight. Musical instruments with shiny finishes and metal strings. Vases and bright glassware. Watches and eyeglasses and elaborately carved figurines. Gorgeous displays of vibrantly hued flowers. Racks of magazines and newspapers.

"I would ask if you're having a good time," Paul said to Fern as he pushed Katy's stroller along the sidewalk, "but your eyes are as bright as a hundred-watt bulb. They tell me you're having a good time."

"I'm havin' a grand time!" she told him. "First of all, I've never ridden in a subway before. Sidhe has nothing like that."

Paul had parked at the outskirts of the city, and the three of them had descended steps that took them belowground. Fern had expected to see some sort of cave dwelling, but what she found were tiled platforms leading to darkened tunnels and tracks. Soon a sleek metal tube had pulled to a stop directly in front of them, and Paul had hurried them onboard. The tram took off like a silver bullet, and before Fern had time to catch her breath, they were in the middle of the city.

"I was worried," Paul said. "You looked frightened when we were in the terminal."

"Not frightened, really." Then she caught his eye and grinned. "Okay, maybe a little. But I knew it was safe or y' wouldn't have let Katy and me go down there. But those tunnels looked awfully dark."

As they passed a doorway, the thick scent of tobacco tickled her nose. She paused to gaze in the window. "Would you look at that," she breathed. She'd seen pipes before. Many of the gnomes and dwarves of Sidhe smoked them. These pipes were made of wood and ivory and other materials she couldn't identify. Many of them were carved into whimsical characters and forest animals. "They're beautiful." She turned to Paul. "Who uses all this...*stuff?* I've seen every manner of goods for sale in the stores. Where I'm from, there are shopkeepers, but they only sell practical things. Bread and cheese. Shoes. Soap. Toothbrushes."

One of Paul's shoulders lifted. "The impractical can become practical when there are millions of people with money to spend."

Fern let the information sink in. Trying to get her mind around it, she repeated, "Millions."

He said, "People have come from practically every country in the world to live and work here. Items that might seem excessive or flamboyant or unnecessary to you and me might be essential to someone else who comes from a different culture."

Fern nodded. Paul made the apparent hedonism sound quite normal, and after hearing his explanation, she guessed it was normal, at that.

Katy struggled against the straps that held her in the stroller. Fern bent and calmed her with a smile. "I think someone's getting hungry."

The three of them went into a deli to purchase sandwiches, juice and chips, and then they walked to a place Paul called Central Park to eat.

They found a shady spot, and Fern spread out a

small blanket Paul had packed in the diaper bag. With sunlight dappling the green grass all around them, they sat and ate.

"I just can't get over it," Fern said. "A huge forest right in the middle of these huge buildings. It's amazing."

Paul told her how, as a boy, he would make trips to New York City with his mother to shop. His father had deplored the crowds and congestion, but his mother had loved the city. Being among the hustling people seemed to invigorate her, and she appreciated the opportunity to sample foods from so many different cultures, from Italian to Turkish to Indian to Cajun.

After they finished lunch, Katy toddled out into the sunlight and Paul went after her. Fern was content to rest in the shade, leaning against the tree trunk and watching them play in the distance.

She felt relaxed and cradled in a drowsy state when the hairs on the back of her neck stood on end. Every sense came alive, and she was suddenly alert.

Something was wrong. She could feel it.

She saw that Paul and Katy were fine, so she began to search the area around her. That's when she felt it…the buzz that whizzed past her head. She shivered and felt a powerful urge to follow whatever it was that had just flown by.

Calming her racing heart, Fern tried to tell herself it was nothing. A flying insect. A hummingbird. But it had been neither—she knew it down to the marrow of her bones. This had been something magical, she was certain. Something a lot like herself.

She vaulted up from the ground, and after a furtive

glance to check that Paul and Katy were still occupied with their fun, she slipped off down the path that led farther into the thick stand of trees.

Soon the foliage became lush, impenetrable to rays of the sun. The temperature was several degrees cooler. Keeping her gaze keen, Fern scanned the ground and the treetops. She wasn't certain what she was looking for, or if—in human form—she'd even be able to see the magical creature if she were to find it. All she knew was that she had to try. Something deep within her told her so.

Then she heard it, that heartrending sound. Her shoulders slumped and every cell in her body grieved. There was nothing on this earth more pitiful than the sound of a pixie crying.

Fern's search became frantic now. What was a pixie doing in Central Park? she wondered. And what had happened to make her weep?

Pixies were happy creatures. They lived and played through each day in joyous abandon. They rarely felt gloomy. Rarely were touched by sadness. But when they were, it was an agonizing sight to behold.

"Hello?" she called toward the treetops. "Where are you?"

The unearthly sobbing stopped.

"Let me help you," Fern said.

She went from one tree to another, scanning the leafy branches.

"I know you're here," she called softly. "Please come down."

A man jogged by, his expression conveying that he thought she wasn't quite right in the head. Embarrassment made her face flush with heat.

She guessed talking to an invisible entity would seem a little bizarre to a human.

Once the man had disappeared around the bend in the path, Fern glanced up into the trees again. She listened intently, but all she heard was birdsong and the leaves being gently rustled by the soft breeze.

However, her skin continued to tingle with awareness. And she still felt a deep and forlorn woe.

A pixie was nearby, and she was in some kind of terrible distress. But if the pixie wasn't willing to accept the help Fern offered, there wasn't much she could do about it.

She glanced through the trees in the direction from which she'd come. Paul would be worried, she knew. She'd left their picnic spot without saying a word to him. But she couldn't leave without making one more attempt to reach out to the pixie.

"Please let me help you," she said. "I'm just like you. I may not look it, but I am."

The tickly sensation was gone. So was the pixie. Fern sighed. She retraced her steps down the narrow path, feeling unsettled by the experience.

"There you are," Paul said when she emerged into the sunlight. "I wondered where you'd gone off to."

"I...I took a little walk," Fern stammered.

He was strapping a slumbering Katy in her stroller.

"She's so funny." Paul was talking about his daughter. He kissed Katy on the temple, then stood to face Fern. "She's ripping and tearing around, and the next thing I know she's zonked out on my shoulder."

He rubbed his palms together. "Well, should we

get this mess packed up? There's plenty more I want you to see.''

"Sure," she told him. "I want to see everythin' there is to see.''

He chuckled. "It would take quite a few trips to see it all, but we'll do the best we can today, okay?''

Fern just smiled as she helped him gather up the wrappers and empty juice containers. Then they folded the blanket and stowed it in the diaper bag.

"Ready?" he asked when the area was clean.

She nodded. But as they walked away, Fern looked back over her shoulder. There was a pixie in that park. And she was terribly unhappy for some reason. She could be lost and all alone. She could be frightened or hurt.

It was with great reluctance that Fern left the pixie behind.

Chapter Six

"Okay." Paul walked into the family room and announced, "I'm ready now."

Fern looked up from where she'd been thumbing through a glossy magazine. "Ready?" she asked. "Ready for what?"

It had been two days since their exciting adventure in New York City. Their lives had settled back into the normal routine. Fern watched Katy during the day while Paul worked on his novel. In the evenings they would have dinner together. Paul would play with Katy or the three of them would take a walk, and then the toddler would be put to bed. Paul had just returned from tucking in his daughter for the night.

"I've got my plot all laid out," he said. "But now I need some secondary characters. I've got the human ones fleshed out, I think. But now I'm ready for you to tell me more about the magical beings of Irish folklore."

"Ah." She smiled, closing the cover of the magazine and sliding it onto the couch cushion beside her. "You want to know more about Sidhe."

"I do." He sat on the chair, his knee nearly contacting hers. "I thought I might have someone—or maybe I should say some*thing*—coming to my protagonist's aid. Something…some being that helps my leading character escape the dullahan."

"But there is no escaping the dullahan," she whispered helplessly, even though she knew he was already privy to the fact.

"I know that. And as I said, in the end the dullahan does succeed in completing the chore of taking my main character to the netherworld." His eyes lit with excitement, his mouth quirking. "But not until the 'dude of death' has been taken on a merry chase first." Paul rubbed his palms together and chuckled. "I was thinking of using a leprechaun as the person…or thing, rather, that helps my guy elude the dullahan for a time."

"A leprechaun is a fairy," she informed him. "A leprechaun would be highly insulted if he heard you call him a thing."

Paul's dark eyes sparked with laughter. "I do apologize to all leprechauns everywhere."

After taking a moment to ponder, Fern said, "I'm not certain a leprechaun would suit your purposes. They're very industrious beings. They take their work too seriously to help a mere mortal with a problem. Leprechauns would see it as a complete waste of time. A cluricaun, maybe, if you could catch one sober."

Curiosity etched Paul's handsome features.

"Cluricauns," she continued, "are related to leprechauns but are not fond of work. They are, however, fond of drink. And mischief. They jump on the backs of unsuspecting animals and ride the terrorized beasts through the night over hill and dale.'' She grinned, admitting, ''There are some who say that cluricauns are leprechauns who cut loose and carouse at midnight, and who refuse to take responsibility for their actions in the sober light of morning.''

He laughed, and the delicious sound made Fern's toes curl.

''Your best bet would probably be a pixie. W— they're—'' she stumbled over the pronoun, nearly saying *we're* ''—known for playing pranks, but it's widely known that pixies have a fondness for mortals. Pixies are curious, and although interfering in the human realm is strictly forbidden, it has been known to happen.''

''A pixie, hmm?'' He looked thoughtful.

''Sprites or brownies might work, too,'' she suggested, eager to move the subject to some other fairy. ''They're usually busy guarding and protecting the forests of Sidhe, but if you created a renegade…'' She didn't finish the thought, thinking it best to let his own imagination take the reins.

''A renegade sprite.''

His handsome countenance assumed a faraway expression, and Fern got the impression that he might have been physically sitting near her in his family room in New York, but his mind, his thoughts, his imagination had slipped off into the story he was creating.

''Maybe the sprite had been helped in the past,''

he murmured, "by a human, and now he's looking to return the favor."

A thought struck her and she blurted, "Will-o'-the-wisps would surely work. They've been called fairy lights. They roam the bogs to help search for the lost."

He nodded, murmuring, "I do intend to include a scene where he gets lost in a misty marsh."

"There are so many fairies, Paul. The banshee, quicklings, elves, gnomes. The Lianhan Shee."

This uncommon name had him blinking back to reality. "And what is that?"

"The love fairy," Fern told him.

His eyebrows arched. "That sounds interesting."

Fern offered a dubious look. "If you think being a love slave is interesting, perhaps. The Lianhan Shee not only seeks love from mortal man. She seeks total dominion over him. It's rare that a man is found who can resist her. And once a man falls prey to her wiles, it's nearly always his ruin."

Once again his luscious dark eyes glazed over, and Fern knew that Paul's mind was churning up ways to fit this fairy into his work. She'd always been content with being a pixie in Sidhe; however, she couldn't help but wonder what his gaze would look like if he were to contemplate her as intensely. Would his eyes go all glassy? Would his thoughts turn chaotic? Or might his brain become so overwhelmed by her that it simply shut down and ceased to function? The mere notion had Fern suppressing a wicked smile.

Then something odd began to happen inside her. She was filled with a peculiar gloominess. She didn't like knowing he was thinking of the Lianhan Shee.

She felt covetous of Paul's thoughts. The love fairy had no right taking up space in Paul's imagination.

Wanting to get Paul's mind off the dangerous and dominating fairy, Fern said, "You know which fairy might make a wonderful villain for a future book?"

Her question snapped Paul to attention. She enjoyed it when he looked at her with such keen interest.

"Which one?" he asked.

"Far Darrig," she told him. "The Red Man. He's related to leprechauns, yet every bone in his body is evil. He gets his name from the way he dresses. From his hat to his cap to his woolen stockings, he's clothed in red. He is amused by mortal terror. He'd make a very nasty villain." She wrinkled her nose. "To make matters worse, his breath is atrocious. Smells like rotten flesh."

She'd lit the fire of his imagination yet again. Fern was pleased to know it was the smelly, tallowy-skinned Far Darrig that had captured Paul's thoughts and not the beautiful love fairy. The Lianhan Shee could only mean trouble for him, anyway, Fern mused.

Paul scooted to the edge of the chair. "Fern, as much as I love hearing your stories of Sidhe, I've got a dozen ideas floating around in my head and I'd like to go jot them down before I lose them. Would you think it rude of me if I were to go work for a couple of hours?"

Before she could respond, his face expressed bewilderment and his forehead creased. "Hold on a second. When I came in here to ask you to tell me about Irish fairies, you said something about Sidhe." He paused, pondering. "You said, 'you want to know more about Sidhe.' Is that what the fairy world is called? But didn't you tell me early on that your hometown is called Sidhe?"

Fern's blood ran cold. *Oh, by me heart,* she swore silently. *What have I done now?*

"Coincidence," she uttered without thought. "Mere coincidence."

He relaxed, nodded. "Knowing your place of birth shares its name with that of the fairy kingdom sure makes your village sound more quaint than ever. I'd like to go for a visit sometime."

She was able to smile, but her gaze dipped away from his.

Paul stood up. "So...do you mind if I go work for a while? I hate to leave you alone this evening, but..."

"Your work is calling your name," she finished for him softly. "It's okay. I understand." Grinning, she added, "I can almost hear your name bein' whispered, meself."

He smoothed the flat of his palms on his muscular thighs. "I can hear it, plain as day."

"You know," she said before he could move toward the door, "that book of yours is somewhat like a fairy. It weaves its spell over you and you can't resist."

His smile flashed white, then the air seemed to settle around them like fairy dust, and he murmured, "You weave a pretty overwhelming spell, yourself."

He held her gaze for one breathless moment before he turned and walked out of the room.

Fern sat in the silence for several minutes before

her heart rate returned to normal. She liked being able to help Paul with his work. She loved that he enjoyed hearing her talk about Sidhe.

The memory of that close call regarding Sidhe's name had her eyes growing wide. She needed to be more careful.

Sidhe hovered in her thoughts. Placing her elbow on the armrest, she unwittingly lifted her hand and pressed her fingers against her mouth.

The place where she lived as a pixie was an enchanted paradise. As a pixie, she could see and feel the pulsating energy being emitted from the lush trees and shrubs. The flowers seemed more vibrantly hued. The sky looked bluer and clear as crystal. The birdsong sounded sweeter, more melodious.

Yes, there was evil lurking about in her magical homeland. But she was able to avoid the most persnickety of the malevolent fairies.

And friends! She had so many pixie friends to have fun with. They flew around Sidhe, happy and carefree. They drank nectar from the flowers, ate fruits and nuts from the trees, explored the countryside. They even ventured out among the hustling, bustling humans once in a while. Life as a pixie was an easy, blissful existence. No worries and few fears.

Normally.

The pixie in Central Park pushed her way into Fern's thoughts. In her mind, Fern could hear the distressing cries all over again, and her heart ached. She wished there had been something she could do, but she couldn't think of a single thing. All she ended up feeling was helpless.

For the benefit of her own mental state, she nudged

thoughts of the troubled pixie aside for now, focusing on Paul's world. The mortal dominion.

She'd so enjoyed her time here in America. Katy was a delight. As a pixie, Fern had loved buzzing around the toddler and making her giggle with delight. But as a human, Fern had been able to dance with Katy, pick her up and swing her around in circles. She loved the feel of Katy's pudgy little hand in hers. And rocking her to sleep, cradling the child in her arms, filled Fern with tender, caring affection that warmed her heart.

The mortal realm held just as much excitement as Sidhe, if the truth were to be told. There was so much to see and do. So much to experience. The delicious food alone was reason enough to want to stay here forever and a day.

But...humans couldn't stay anywhere forever and a day. The facts and consequences of mortality made that impossible. In Sidhe, pixies, sprites, gnomes, elves, all the fairies were ageless, and time seemed to go on forever.

The idea of agelessness had her wondering just how old she was. She had no idea, really. She could be a hundred years old or three hundred years old. She had no way of knowing.

Why, she thought, had she become human at the age she had? What her human age was, she couldn't be certain of, either. But having seen pictures of Maire around the house, Fern felt she could safely judge herself to be in Maire's age bracket.

It wasn't as if she'd ever consciously thought about what age to become. She simply...had become. So why hadn't she turned into a human child so she could entertain Katy, or a wizened old woman who could offer Paul sage advice? Why had she metamorphosed into a human female who was about the same age as Paul's deceased wife?

A whispery voice in the back of her head told her she shouldn't be pondering these questions. That the answers could hold some dire consequences.

She didn't have a problem veering her thoughts away from the troubling queries. However, she was helpless when it came to reflections of Paul.

He was the epitome of the human world for her. The emotions he sparked in her were overwhelming. Attempting to describe them left her feeling at a loss. There simply weren't words to express how he made her feel. All she could say was that the emotions were incomparable to anything…ever.

Fern sat for the longest time comparing and contrasting Sidhe and the world mortals took for reality. In the end she could only come to one conclusion: Paul's human realm won out, hands down.

After lunch the next day, Paul took a break from his work and joined Fern and Katy for a walk. Fern basked in the hot rays of the sun, lifting her face to them.

"It's a beautiful day," she said.

"Boooo-tiful," Katy parroted, walking between the adults, one hand held by Fern, the other by her father.

Looking down, Fern saw that the toddler was mimicking her, her chubby-cheeked face tipped skyward. Fern chuckled, and when her gaze met Paul's, she noticed he had a curious look in his eye, an expression that held such heavy intensity that it caused her breath to catch.

"What is it?" she asked.

"It's you." He paused, then said, "It's just as Katy said. You're boooo-tiful."

His imitation of Katy made her grin, but his compliment made her blood rush through her veins.

"Your daughter was talkin' about the day," she pointed out. "About the weather." She spread her free arm out wide. "About this glorious sunshine."

"Well, she was right just the same."

Fern's heart skipped behind her ribs.

"You do like the outdoors, don't you?" he asked.

"What's not to like?" she fired back lightly. "The air is so fresh. The flowers smell like heaven. The trees are lush and green. Even the fragrance of the cut grass is lovely."

He walked for several steps seeming to be in deep contemplation. But it wasn't long before she felt his attention fall on her once again, and her entire being was jarred from the heat of it.

"I like the fact that you enjoy everything so much," he said. "You put your whole heart into getting the most out of every moment, whether it's spent taking a simple walk down a country road or touring a huge city. It's clear that you truly enjoy the time you spend with Katy—" his tone lowered an octave "—and with me."

The velvety timbre of his voice set off a chain reaction in Fern. Her pulse pattered, her belly tightened, and a shiver coursed through her being. She was so glad they were out in the heat of the sun's rays, otherwise, she was sure goose bumps would have popped up on her arms. This man made her react. Whether it was with words, a look or a touch, her body never failed to respond to him.

"Savor every adventure," she said, shocked by how rusty the words sounded to her own ears.

He nodded. "You truly live by that motto, don't you? I guess what I'm so envious of is that you view every experience as an adventure."

"Every experience *is* an adventure, Paul," she said.

"Yes, but what I've discovered over the course of my life is that most 'adventures' are fairly mundane. My days raising Katy are pretty much the same. The sun comes up, the sun goes down. Nothing out of the ordinary happens in between."

She stopped and turned to face him. "Oh, I don't agree with that at all. Every day with Katy brings something new and amazing. Yesterday she stacked six blocks in a tower all by herself. She was so pleased! The look of accomplishment on her face made my spirits soar. And just this morning she stopped all of a sudden and her eyes went wide, and she proudly announced she was making pee-pee."

Paul brightened, his shoulders squaring with obvious pride, and he looked down at his little girl. "I think she's ready for some potty training."

"I think she is." Fern grinned. "Now won't *that* be an adventure!"

His laugh was free and easy, and the airy feeling it gave Fern made her feel as if she could take flight. She knew gravity was too much for her as a human, but she really liked this buoyant feeling.

However, his glee faded quickly. "Fern, I don't know a thing about potty-training a toddler."

"Oh, come on now," she gently chided. "Don't let that spoil the fun of it. I've never trained a child, either, but how hard can it be? You take off her diaper and sit her on the pot. She'll get the idea soon enough, I expect."

He studied her for a moment, that peculiar intensity rearing its head again, and then he remarked, "You know, you're right. I need to start savoring every adventure. Even potty training."

"There y' go," she told him happily. "That's the spirit!"

They walked a bit more, and then Paul said, "Maybe we should start back. It'll be time for her nap soon."

"It will," Fern agreed.

The three of them started back toward the house, when a car came around the bend. Automatically they inched closer to the side of the road. A streak of fur shot out from the tall grass, racing directly into the car's path.

"Fluffy!" Fern called.

Katy's cry was drowned out by the sound of tires screeching against the asphalt. Every muscle in Fern's body tensed, and instinct alone had her reaching for Katy and swooping the toddler up securely in her arms. The driver of the car swerved, but was unable to keep from striking the animal. Fluffy yowled as he went rolling, then lay still where he landed at the opposite side of the roadway.

Paul shot across the street and knelt by the cat.

The air went eerily still, and Fern's stomach was

doing flip-flops. The whole scene had seemed to take place in slow motion, yet it had all happened in the span of a heartbeat.

The driver jumped out of the car and approached Paul. "Hey, mister—" the teenage boy's eyes were wide with fear "—is that your cat? I tried to stop. I'm sorry. I'm really, really sorry."

"It was an accident," Paul said. "My cat ran right out in front of you. I saw that. There was no way you could stop in time."

The boy looked down at Fluffy. "Is it okay?"

Paul didn't answer, just stared down at the too-still animal. Then he looked over at Fern. The angst straining his features tugged at her.

"Paul?" she said. Her tone held questions that she wasn't even sure she wanted answers to.

"Fluffy sweeping?" Katy patted Fern's cheek to get her attention. Fern tried hard to smile at the child. Fat, fearful tears watered the toddler's eyes.

"I don't know, Katy," Fern whispered.

"He's alive," Paul announced. "But he's hurt. He needs to see the vet. Right away."

"I have a blanket in my trunk," the teen offered. "I'll be happy to drive you to the vet. Can I stay with you to see if your cat is okay?"

Paul nodded. "Sure. And I could use the blanket to wrap him in. Keeping him warm might help with the shock."

While the boy went to the back of the car, Paul crossed the road to Fern and Katy.

"Honey—" he smoothed his fingers over Katy's cheek, whisked away a tear with the pad of his thumb "—I'm going to take Fluffy to see the doctor. I don't want you to worry. Everything will be okay. You stay with Fern.''

In response Katy hugged Fern around the neck and buried her face against her shoulder.

''She'll probably take a nap,'' Fern told him. ''Don't worry about us. We'll be fine.'' Her brow puckered. ''Do you think Fluffy will be okay?''

He pursed his lips and took a deep breath. Finally he murmured, ''He's breathing, but I can't honestly say for sure if he'll make it.''

Then he did the most extraordinary thing. He leaned forward and kissed her cheek. His lips were warm against her skin, and Fern's chest ached with the sweetness of his touch. Something in her told her this intimate contact between humans—between a man and a woman who cared for each other—was part of the secret she so longed to learn.

''I'll be home just as soon as I can,'' he promised, then he turned and walked away.

He took the blanket from the boy and ever so gently wrapped Fluffy in it. He picked up the cat and then rounded the car and got in. They drove away, leaving Fern and Katy standing there on the road.

Sadness and worry seemed to flood Fern's body, turning her blood to sludge. Being human was *hard*, she decided right then and there. Dealing with pain and agony and...the fear of death. Her knees felt quaky as she hugged Katy to her.

She had learned that humans experienced much happiness. They shared a concern for each other that led to...other things. Intimate and cozy feelings. Yes, there were some wonderful aspects to being mortal. However, there were difficulties, too. Complications and unforeseen tragedies that could catch you unawares, that could turn your joy to sorrow before you even had time to reach for your bag of pixie dust.

Fern sighed. As a human, she didn't have the luxury of having a bag of magical dust.

"Come on, sweetums," she crooned. "Let's go home."

Even the bright sunshine wasn't enough to lighten the darkness that filled her as she carried Katy down the road. But then she thought about the feel of Paul's kiss against her cheek, and how it had provoked in her a profound yearning for more.

Something inside her—some force she couldn't name—strengthened to the point that her spine actually straightened, and she walked taller suddenly.

Fern realized that all the doubtful and anxious feelings she'd experienced while being human would be worth it, if she were to get the chance to stay with Paul forever.

But just as quickly as the strength inflated in her, it collapsed. She wasn't human. Well, not normally, she wasn't. She was only enjoying this flesh-and-blood body due to magic. She was a pixie, that's what she needed to remember. And pixies belonged in Sidhe.

Anything else was pure fantasy.

She'd already come to the conclusion that Paul needed someone. A real human someone. A woman who could share the joys in his life. A woman who could help him through the tough times. What Fern needed to remember was that she could only stay here long enough to convince Paul of that.

Chapter Seven

"I am so sorry."

The young man who sat in the vet's waiting room with Paul must have apologized at least a dozen times. The teen's name was Donny Roberts, and this had only been the second time he'd taken the car out for a drive on his own. The car belonged to his parents, and Paul had insisted that Donny call home to let his mom and dad know what happened and where he was.

"It's going to be all right," Paul assured him, even though he wasn't at all convinced Fluffy would pull through.

Donny glanced over at the closed door of the exam room. "How long do you think it will be before they tell us something? It's not that I want to go." Worry contorted his young face. "I really want to stay. It's just that I'm nervous. I hope your cat doesn't..."

"It shouldn't be long now." But Paul had no idea

if he was lying to the boy or telling the truth. There was just no way to say.

They fell silent. However, with a background of mewing and barking of the animals waiting to be seen by the veterinarian, Paul found himself pondering the blond-haired, blue-eyed teen. What kind of kid was he? What kind of home did he come from? How did his parents treat him?

It was the writer's curse. This constant wondering about the lives of others.

Obviously, Donny's parents had raised a conscientious kid. It would have been very easy for the boy to simply drive on after he'd struck Fluffy. But this young man possessed a superior character. He had immediately expressed regret, and hadn't hesitated to help get the animal to the vet's office.

Paul worried about Katy. His daughter would be quite upset if her kitty didn't come home. He wondered how distraught she was right now. The fact that Fern was with her eased Paul's mind.

Ah, Fern.

Paul feared that his heart was in jeopardy. He couldn't believe all the ways the woman had touched his life since they had met. She honestly cared about his daughter. She had helped him to see that every aspect of life with Katy could be a true adventure. And she'd helped him hurdle the barrier that had kept him from writing.

She had brightened his world.

That's exactly what she had done. That's exactly what she *was*.

A beautiful and radiant light.

However, she was sweet…and oh, so innocent. She

deserved to experience her first intimate relationship
with someone who could look at love with the same
freshness, the same excitement, the same newness and
sparkle as she did.

It wasn't that Fern didn't excite him. Lord, help
him! She excited him plenty. He simply felt she deserved someone...else.

Having been married before, he'd been blessed
with his chance at that first-love feeling. And being a
widower, he'd suffered a grief so deep that he was
reluctant to give his heart completely again. Fern really was worthy of—

Just then the door of the exam room opened, and
the grim-faced vet beckoned to him.

Paul got out of the car and shut the door. He bent
down and leaned toward the open window. "Thanks
for bringing me home," he told the boy.

Donny opened his mouth to speak, but Paul cut him
off. "No more apologizing. You heard the doctor.
Things could have been much worse had you not gotten Fluffy to the vet as quickly as you did." He
pointed a friendly finger at the teen. "I've got your
phone number. I'll call you and give you an update
on Fluffy as soon as I know something."

Gratitude lit the young man's blue eyes. "Thanks,
Mr. Roland."

Paul stepped away from the car, and Donny lifted
his hand in farewell before driving off down the long
lane.

Fern met him at the door, and Paul felt light and
buoyant the moment he laid eyes on her.

"How's Katy?" he asked.

"Poor little tyke cried herself to sleep, she did."
Apprehension darkened Fern's eyes to an intriguing
deep aquamarine. "How is Fluffy?"

"He'll be fine," he told her. "They had to operate.
One of his hind legs was broken. And the vet had to
use several pins to fix a broken hip. They wanted to
keep him a few days for observation."

Powerful emotion emanated from her in waves.
Tears welled up in her eyes, and he saw the nearly
imperceptible tremble of her delicate chin.

"I didn't know what to do." A fat tear slid down
her cheek. "I felt so helpless. I tried to console Katy.
Her tears broke my heart. She seems too young to
understand what was going on, but she sure was upset."

Paul could relate. Fern's tears were breaking his
heart right now.

"I sang to her," she continued. "Rocked her. Tried
to get her mind off Fluffy with a book, with toys, but
nothing worked. Finally she just exhausted herself
and fell asleep."

Regret walloped Paul. "I'm sorry I couldn't be
here with you." He placed his hands on her shoulders.

The instant he touched her he knew he'd made a
drastic mistake. The very air seemed to coagulate to
the point that he couldn't draw in a breath. The universe seemed to shrink in around them until there was
nothing in existence except the two of them.

The anxiety left her eyes wide, and her full, lush
lips parted. He knew she had no idea how tantalizing
her mouth was to him.

"You couldn't be here," she whispered. "I knew

that. Fluffy was hurt. Someone had to take care of Katy's pet.''

He slid his hands down her arms, cupping her elbows in his palms.

''I was so relieved that you were here with her.'' His voice grated. ''I'm grateful to you for cuddling her through her distress.''

They may have been talking about his daughter and the accident, but Paul knew without a doubt that it was something else entirely that was making his words sound raspy...something that was so potent that it was nearly strangling him.

One of his hands seemed to lift of its own volition. Her cheek was warm and soft against his fingertips, like a silky, sun-kissed flower petal. His fingers trailed along her cheekbone, traced the graceful outline of her ear. He took its lobe between his index finger and thumb. For the first time, he noticed that she wasn't wearing earrings, that her perfect little ears weren't even pierced. He realized that he'd never seen her wear any kind of jewelry at all.

However, her burnished curls were more glorious and shiny than the purest of spun gold. Fern didn't need baubles and precious metals of adornment. She was dangerously alluring without those normal womanly frills.

A tiny voice in the back of his head whispered a warning.

''I can't do this,'' he said just as the thought passed through his mind.

''Of course y' can,'' she murmured. ''Of course y' can.''

As if it were some sort of incantation, the phrase

she repeated wound and curled around him, drowning out the cautionary notions that raced in his brain.

Of course he could. Of course he could.

Ever so slowly, he leaned down and placed a chaste kiss on her luscious mouth. He pulled back a fraction of an inch, felt her sweet breath on his skin when she gasped softly. He touched her lips with his once again, surrendering to the urge to taste her.

She was velvet under his tongue. Hot sweetness. And he stifled the groan that rose in the back of his throat.

The scent of her teased him. The taste of her nearly brought him to his knees. His hold on control was tentative at best and was wavering with each passing second.

He hadn't wanted to do this. He had only the best intentions for her and her first intimate experience. He should pull away. He really shouldn't be doing this.

Of course you should. Of course you should.

He had no idea if she actually spoke the words, or if the spell was now being chanted by his own traitorous impulses...his own selfish desires. He felt drunk with the wanting that throbbed through his body.

Eyes closed, every cell in him calling out a demand for more, he let his mouth hover a whisper's breath from hers.

"Th-this." She purred tenderly. "It's part of the secret, isn't it? I can feel it in me bones. I want your hands on me. I want your lips on mine. Your skin touching mine."

He didn't dare tell her all that *he* wanted.

"Fern, we really need to—"

"Shhhh. Don't speak. Don't say another word."

And then she did the most astonishing thing. She lifted up on tiptoe and pressed her mouth to his. She combed her fingers through his hair, pulled him to her tightly. She parted her lips, and her tongue flicked out to taste him. Paul felt it was the most erotic experience he'd ever had…to think that one so innocent could act so brazen.

The full length of her body was tight against his, and he feared she would feel the hardness of his desire. He wanted to put some space between them, but he couldn't seem to move. Couldn't seem to think. Couldn't seem to act. All he could do was stand there and…*feel*.

Her mouth worked over his, suckling, her teeth nipping, her tongue dancing in languid circles. He couldn't say when he'd lost control over the moment. He had thought he'd been the one in command. But she'd stolen his thunder. She'd overthrown his rule, his power, and heaven help him, but he was more than willing to be conquered.

She ran her hand down the side of his face, then along the length of his neck. Her touch was slow and lazy and tormenting as the hounds from hell. He wanted to wrest control from her, seize the moment, bend her to his will, take her…*have* her. But he only stood there, taking pleasure in her kiss, enjoying her touch.

The heat of her skin scorched him through the thin cotton fabric of her top. He slid his hands over her back, hugging her to him.

Her kiss was electric. Like lightning. Like thunder. All rolled into one.

Evidently, natural impulses alone had her breaking contact with his lips and feathering kisses along his jaw, her teeth pinching down with excruciating pleasure on his earlobe, her open mouth tasting his heated flesh. It must have been instinct driving her. He knew she was too innocent to know the havoc she was wreaking on him, mind and body.

Some innate, deeply ingrained carnal spurring must have compelled her to slide her hand down. Her palm splayed at the waistband of his trousers—his stomach tightening in response—and slowly she smoothed her way farther southward.

He inhaled sharply, his eyes opening wide when he finally realized her destination. He gently encircled her wrist with his fingers.

"Fern. Wait."

"I can't wait any longer, Paul." Her nicely rounded breasts rose and fell with her accelerated breath. "I want the secret. And I want it now."

He silently prayed. He was going to need a band of angels to rescue him from her innocent yet insanely erotic determination.

She was angry with him. And she didn't care that she'd been pouting like a spoiled brat for two days. She'd gotten so close to the secret. She knew she had. Something deep in her being told her so. The look in Paul's eyes told her so. The strange and mysterious current swimming around them told her so, too.

Fern threw back the covers and got out of bed.

Morning sunlight streamed through the window, and she stretched and yawned.

Suddenly she stopped. She was human. She'd gone to bed human. And she'd awakened that way, too. She hadn't been sure before, but she was sure this morning.

Most nights Fern had a blast as a pixie, chasing the lightning bugs and startling the tree frogs and dancing on the flower petals. She'd somersault and spin and twist in loop-de-loops through the silky night air.

But since that kiss—since she'd experienced those awesome emotions—everything had changed. Everything was different.

She'd spent her days and her nights pondering the feel of Paul's lips against hers, the scent of his cologne, the feel of his hair between her fingers, the taste of his skin on her tongue, the hardness of his body against hers. Oh, she was paying close attention to Katy when she was responsible for the tot, but Fern looked forward to the time when Paul came out of his study late every day. She found herself checking the door of his office several times throughout each afternoon to see if he still had the world—and her— closed out.

Then there were the nights. During the long dark hours spent lying awake in her bed, she'd dream of that kiss. She'd relive it. Fantasize about it. Do everything she could to recreate those wondrous feelings. The notion of becoming a pixie and flying through the night never entered her head. And once she fell asleep, she reveled in the sweet dreams of Paul that filled her mind. Smoky, hungry visions that stirred her deeply…intensely.

However, she always awoke feeling miffed. She wanted that secret, darn it. She knew kissing was part of it. But she wanted the rest. She wanted it all.

But just when she'd let her emotions take over, when they had shared that luscious kiss, Paul had caught her hand in his and forced himself away from her.

He hadn't wanted to. The planes and angles of his handsome face had been tense with regret. Yet even though he'd found it difficult, he'd called a halt to the cozy moment of delicious enjoyment—and that had peeved Fern to no end!

It wasn't that she expected some kind of lifetime commitment from him or anything. That was impossible. She knew that. She had to return to Sidhe, and she planned to do that just as soon as she talked to Paul about finding a mate for himself…a woman with whom he could share life's troubles and tribulations, joys and delight.

But just because she meant to return to Ireland didn't mean he couldn't send her home a little more… enlightened.

And he hadn't even given her much in the way of an excuse this time, either. Before, he'd tried to explain that he felt he wasn't the right person with whom she should explore the secrets of intimacy. But after they had kissed, he'd simply studied her face and then walked away. His reaction had baffled her…and frustrated her to high heaven.

Closing her eyes, Fern concentrated on the blue denim skirt and white cotton shirt hanging in her closet. She focused her thoughts on each detail of the outfit, willing it onto her body. When she opened her eyes, however, she saw that she still wore her loose-fitting pale-blue sleep shift.

She clenched her eyes shut and focused with single-minded concentration on the clothing. But when she raised her eyelids, she wasn't wearing the skirt and top.

Her head hammered as she trudged over to the closet to retrieve the outfit. Every other day she'd been able to change her clothes just by thinking about it, but today she couldn't. And it had been days since she'd even thought about metamorphosing into her pixie form. What was happening to her? Was she losing the magic that was so available in the fairy world?

Panic flushed her face with a thin sheen of perspiration. What would she do if she couldn't return to Sidhe? If she could never again sprout wings and fly high above the treetops?

She'd be trapped. Forever bound to the human world. She'd be far away from her beloved Sidhe. Unable to return. Ever.

Her sorrowful musing had her thinking about the Central Park pixie. The mournful creature who was lost and alone. Any pixie worth her salt would find some way to help one of her own who was in need. Fern had to do something. She needed to find the lost pixie and see why she wailed so desolately.

Katy called out, and Fern knew another busy day had begun.

There was so much to do, so much to think about. The Central Park pixie weighed on her mind. But before Fern could help anyone, she had to find some way to help herself. She needed to talk to Paul. And she needed to find a bit of time alone to test her magic…see if she could become a pixie, or if she'd lost the ability altogether.

"Oh, by me heart," she whispered. She hoped and prayed she hadn't lost her power.

"My Fwuffy!"

When Paul carried the furry cat in through the back door, Katy's face lit up with utter delight. The child toddled over, reaching and straining for the animal. Fluffy's long, puffy tail cut a wide swath through the air.

"Listen, sweetie," Paul warned his daughter. "We need to be very careful with Fluffy for a while. He's got boo-boos that need to heal. Okay?"

He bent down and let Katy stroke Fluffy's fur. The cat purred loudly. Clearly, the animal was happy to be home.

After getting herself dressed for the day—in the all-too-human way of doing it, stripping out of one garment and donning another—Fern had sought out Paul to talk to him. She wanted to tell him her thoughts about his finding someone to share his life with. She also needed to explain that it was time for her to go home.

However, he'd already sequestered himself in his office by the time she'd dressed Katy and fed her a bit of breakfast. When he had come out late that afternoon, he told her he'd called the vet and learned that Fluffy was ready to come home. Katy had been elated by the news. Fern had been happy to know the cat was getting better, but she was so darned preoccupied with her fretfulness; every time she thought

about losing her ability to become a pixie, panic
soaked her thoroughly like a summer shower.

She'd done her best to push it from her mind, realizing that worrying wasn't going to help matters.
There was nothing she could do about her suspicions
until she could be completely alone, and that wouldn't
be possible until Paul could take over the responsibility of watching his daughter. But the sun was low
on the horizon now. Surely he wouldn't want to go
back into his office now.

"Aren't you going to come pet Fluffy?" Paul
asked.

Fern struggled to swim out of the strong current of
anxiety. "Sure," she told him. "I'd like to welcome
the little bugger home."

Once she'd bent down next to Paul, Katy and
Fluffy, Fern saw that the cat was toting a stiff cast on
its hind leg.

"Poor kitty." Fern trailed her fingers over the cat's
soft coat. Fluffy's purring grew louder. Fern looked
at Paul. "Is he in pain?" she asked.

"The vet says no. The cast will be a little cum-
bersome for him. But it won't be for long. Soon he'll
be good as new. However, we do need to keep Fluffy
quiet. He doesn't realize he's hurt, the vet said, and
he'll try to jump and race around if we let him."
Absently, Paul scratched behind the cat's ears. "I
need to call Donny Roberts and let him know the
good news."

Paul's chestnut eyes never wavered from hers.
There was something in his face...something different. A lightness. That tiny little line of tension that

had been between his eyes for days was no longer there.

Fern blinked, wondering if she was imagining it, and she quickly decided she wasn't.

"You look troubled," he commented.

His observation startled her. "Well...I *do* have something on me mind."

"You need to talk? We could chat while I fix dinner."

"I would like to talk, yes," she told him. "But first I need...some time...to..." She let the rest of her thought trail off. She couldn't tell him the honest truth, so she blurted out, "I've had a tense day. And I'd like a bath before we eat. Would you mind watching Katy for a while? I'll be quick about it."

"Take your time." He reached down and ruffled his daughter's hair. "Katy can sit out in the yard with Fluffy while I grill a hamburger. I know you don't eat meat, but—" he grinned ruefully "—I need some beef. I'll make a nice salad for you." His eyes glittered. "She'll be fine. Go have a bath. Read a book. Relax." Then he captured Fern with a riveting gaze. "But I wanted to tell you that I have something on my mind, too. I'd like to talk...later."

Fern felt her mouth form a silent oh, and she felt winded all of a sudden, as if she'd run for miles and miles without a chance to rest.

"You would?" she asked, knowing the question sounded quite inane.

"Just as soon as we can find a few minutes alone."

Katy giggled when Fluffy stretched out on his back to have his belly rubbed, the cast plunking against the floor. But Fern thought the sound of the child's happy laughter and the purring of the cat sounded far off to her ears.

"Go," Paul urged her. "Katy will be okay with me. You've earned a break. We'll have plenty of time to talk later."

But as Fern ascended the stairs to the second floor, she knew time was something that was very quickly dwindling away. There was so much to do, so much to say, and so little time was left for them.

That new look on Paul's face intrigued her, and she couldn't help but wonder what it was all about. And what was it that he wanted to talk to her about? Whatever it was, it must have something to do with the relaxed aura he was projecting today.

In the bathroom she stopped up the tub, turned on the faucet and adjusted the water temperature. Then she began to strip out of her clothes. She didn't even bother trying to use enchantment to undress. She simply couldn't take any more disappointment right now. Every time she imagined that she might have lost her fairy powers, she was bombarded with fear.

What she needed to do was put everything else aside. Push everything—Katy, Fluffy, Paul, *everything*—right out of her mind. Fern was determined to sit in the warm water and gather together every ounce, every shred, every nuance of her magical power. Focusing on herself was all important. She intended to turn back into a pixie. She was desperate to prove to herself that she could. If she succeeded, she would be very happy indeed. If she failed...she sighed...at least she would have a good soaking.

Chapter Eight

Fern reclined in the tub and relaxed every muscle in her body. Even the tiniest movement set the water lapping at her high, rounded breasts, her tummy, her toes. The warm, silky liquid tickled her skin. It was a feeling reminiscent of the tingling sensation she'd felt all over when Paul had kissed her...when his fingers had glided down her arms, roamed over her face.

Paul. His handsome face hovered behind her closed eyelids.

Heat swirled in her, fogging her mind like the thick mists that rose on the Irish moors. It was easy to imagine the feel of his kiss on her lips, the taste of his skin on her tongue, the velvet of his fingertips on her flesh.

Strange things happened to this human body of hers. Her nipples hardened into nubs that were so tight it was almost painful, and her chest rose and fell with more vigor. It was utterly amazing that mere thoughts of Paul could make her feel so...*hot* that bathwater felt tepid against her fiery flesh.

Her reason for slipping away slammed into her head. Her gasp was nearly audible, her eyes opening wide. She had to stop this.

He was the obstacle that kept her from changing. He was like a massive boulder in the middle of the pathway of her life. She'd realized that. Paul was holding her earthbound. She had to put him out of her mind if she wanted to test her pixie powers.

Fern concentrated on Sidhe, closing her eyes and focusing in on her lush and wonderful fairy home. The emerald green of the hills that gently undulated right down into a cerulean sea. She thought of her friends, and immediately her mouth curled into a sprightly grin.

She directed all her thoughts with single-minded deliberation. A powerful current snapped and sparked around her like static electricity. The fine hair on her arms rose, and she felt lighter than air. As her body contracted, she was enveloped in a thousand thin tendrils that plucked and smoothed and eddied around her, picking her up in invisible fingers.

Her wings sprouted from her back like arrows from a bow. Instantly they began to flutter, and when she opened her eyes she was hovering inches above the bathwater.

The first thing she felt was a relief so vast that it was overwhelming. She hadn't lost her power. Turning back into her pixie form hadn't been easy, that was certain. She'd had to concentrate and focus her energies on the task at hand. But she *had* been able to metamorphose.

Glee had her tossing her head back and laughing. "Fern!"

The pounding on the bathroom door and the tone of Paul's voice scared her out of her skin. In the blink of an eye, she was human. She hit the water with a huge splash. Pain shot through her elbows and knees where they impacted the hard porcelain.

"Are you okay?" Paul shouted from the other side of the bathroom door. "You fell? Open the door!"

He jiggled the door handle, and Fern panicked. She sloshed up onto her knees and reached for a towel to cover herself.

"I'm okay," she called. In the back of her mind she had the fleeting thought that, as a pixie, she'd never suffered this strange...what was it? Self-consciousness? Being human came with a healthy— or was it not-so-healthy?—dash of inhibition.

"What's wrong?" she said, stepping out of the tub and drying herself on the towel. "What's happened?"

"It's Katy. She's gone."

Anxiety froze in her veins. "Gone?" She heard him pacing outside the door like a caged changeling while she hurriedly rubbed the towel over her body.

"I only left her in the yard for a moment," he continued. "I forgot to bring out the spatula, so I ran inside to get it. When I came out the back door, she and Fluffy were gone. I called and searched. I need you."

Those three little words affected Fern like no other. Her chest felt heavy with some unidentifiable emotion.

She wrapped the towel securely around her body and opened the door. "Let me get dressed," she told him. "And I'll help y' look for her. She can't have gone far."

Worry clouded his expression, and her heart ached.

"Hurry," he said. "I'll be looking in the paddocks out back. She could be anywhere. She could get hurt. There's so much out there—"

"Stop that this instant," she scolded. "She'll be fine. She's just having an adventure with Fluffy, is all." She waved him away. "Off with y', then. I'll be right out."

Minutes later Fern was searching the dark confines of a shed on Paul's property, calling Katy's name. Fern couldn't believe the babe would go into the dark on her own. But she might follow her limping cat inside. Katy sure did love that animal.

She could hear the faint sound of Paul's frantic voice as he hunted for his daughter farther out in the yard. Then a plaintive mewl made Fern go still. The sound wasn't in the shed at all, but had come from outside, around the back of the building.

Fern backed out of the cluttered shed and called, "Paul! I hear Fluffy!" Then she hurried to investigate. When she rounded the corner of the building, horror and fear made her mouth go cotton dry.

Somehow, Katy had scaled a rickety hay wagon that was parked on a slight incline. She was obviously following Fluffy out onto the hitch where the cat sat, its tail swishing, its broken leg hanging awkwardly over the back edge. Fern marveled that the injured animal had been able to jump up onto the wagon. Each shaky inch Katy scrambled farther out onto the metal hitch, the wagon teetered, its fat rubber wheels rocking from the momentum. It wouldn't take much to set the cart into motion.

"By me heart," Fern whispered under her breath. Katy could be hurt if the wagon suddenly lurched forward. The babe would fall from her precarious perch, of that there was no doubt in Fern's mind. She had a fleeting thought that Fluffy was bound to injure his pinned hip, but the main focus of her fear was Katy. If she fell and the wheels began rolling, the wagon could run right over the child.

Cold sweat broke out on Fern's upper lip.

"Katy—" Fern kept her tone as calm as she could while she made her way toward the wagon "—sweetie, be still a minute."

The toddler giggled. "Pway hide-and-seek, Fun!"

"Hold on," Fern said. "I'm coming to play. Sit very still there. Don't move."

Once she got close, Fluffy leaped off the hitch, landing on the grass with a yowl and scurrying away with a pronounced limp; however, that small burst of force had been enough to set the wagon moving. It rolled down the hill directly at Fern, slowly at first, but quickly gaining speed.

The same terror that widened Katy's eyes also lit a fire in Fern. She fought the awesome urge to flee that welled up seeming out of nowhere, and instead she made a mad dash to meet the wagon. She had no idea what she would do, but she couldn't allow harm to come to that precious wee child.

"Fern!" Paul shouted from somewhere behind her.

Don't look back! a voice in her head screamed. She knew that if she turned around, she and Katy both would be done for. The only other thought that had

time to sough through her head was a plea for help
to all that was holy. She had to save her beloved Katy.

Lifting her hand straight out, she caught the front-
most part of the hitch in the palm of her hand. She
was vaguely aware of the cool, rounded metal against
her skin as she dug her toes into the ground. The laws
of gravity continued to carry Katy forward, and Fern
reached out with her free arm and caught the flying
tot around the waist. Even though Fern's grip was
sure and gentle, young Katy still let out an *oof* as the
breath was knocked from her. Then Katy began to
howl from nothing but pure fear.

Fern stood there holding Katy and the wagon, her
arm muscles quivering with the strain of the weight
of the rickety contraption.

In one smooth motion, Fern shoved the hitch in one
direction and ran like the wind in the other. For an
instant she thought she'd taken flight. But then her
balance went cockeyed, and she feared she would fall
with Katy in her arms. However, she miraculously
remained on her feet and raced to the bottom of the
incline. Then she watched as the wagon crashed into
the side of the shed, the hitch punching a hole right
through the dry and splintery wood.

"Fern—"

Terror etched itself in Paul's tone, in the terse angles of his face.

"—you could have been killed."

He came to her, automatically took his crying child
and comforted her with a hug and soothing hands, but
his eyes were riveted to Fern's.

"You saved Katy's life," he said, his tone husky
with emotion. "You put your own safety aside. You

didn't have to, but you did.'' He looked at the wagon, his dark brows drawing together in a sudden frown. "How did you do that? How did you stop that wagon? That thing must weigh three hundred pounds.''

The realization of it all made Fern's knees buckle. She sat down on the grass and stared at the cart at the bottom of the hill.

Finally, her voice quavering, she admitted, "I don't know, Paul. I honestly don't know.''

Fern knew what she had to do. And there could be no avoiding the inevitable.

She found Paul in the kitchen pouring himself a glass of lemonade. He'd spent most of the evening cuddling with Katy. The near catastrophe had shaken all of them, and Paul had evidently felt the need to spend some time with his daughter. But Katy was upstairs fast asleep in her crib now, and Fern knew it was time for her to deliver her news.

"Would you like some?'' he asked when he noticed she'd come into the room. "We can take it out back, on the patio. It's a nice night.''

"Sure.''

He took down another glass and poured some lemonade for her. She went to the freezer for ice for their drinks.

It didn't escape her notice that, once they went outside, Paul didn't take the adjacent chair, but sat next to her on the lawn settee.

She sipped the sweet, lemony drink and then set the glass on the table. She turned toward Paul. "There's no easy way to say this,'' she began slowly.

"But I have to tell you that it's time for me to go home."

Astonishment had his jaw going slack. "Fern, no. You've been here barely two weeks." He looked away long enough to set his glass down next to hers. Then he faced her again. "I never expected this. I mean, I knew you'd go back to Ireland eventually, but not this soon."

"I don't belong here," she told him. "I only came to help."

Paul replied, "And that's exactly what you've done."

He captured her hand in his, and immediately his touch caused her skin to tingle.

"My daughter has blossomed with you here," he told her. "Katy's happy with you. She's learning new words, learning to communicate better. She's ready to be potty-trained. I'm not saying I'm not a good parent. I love my daughter. You know that. I've always done my best to care for her. But she seems to have learned more, learned quicker, in the weeks that you've been here."

Fern shook her head. "Ah, no. I can't take credit for normal learnin'. Children are inquisitive beings. She's done all that she's done on her own without any help from the likes o' me."

She could tell from his expression that he didn't believe it.

"And you've helped me, too," he said. "You kick-started my creative engine with those wonderful tales of Irish folklore. I've come up with ideas for two more books. That's one of the things I wanted to tell you about tonight."

His rich chestnut eyes lit with excitement when he talked about his writing, and a thrill shot through Fern like a thousand tiny arrows that had been dipped in pure pleasure. She had helped him regain his muse, and that pleased her very much.

"You've helped me become a better father," he continued. "I feel as if I was going through the motions with Katy before. I kept her warm. I kept her fed. But I think I wasn't nurturing her enough emotionally. But now I see that she's a joy, Fern. I love being with her. Love seeing her reaction to things. She's a person. With likes and dislikes and opinions."

A knot rose in Fern's throat.

His gazed took on a sudden intensity. "You've helped me as a man, too, Fern. You've...awakened something in me." His words took on a halting quality, an uncertainty. It seemed as if he was working out the thoughts—voicing them as they came into his head. "Something that's lain dormant for a very long time." He moistened his lips. Swallowed. "I told myself, told everyone...that I had gotten over Maire's death. That I wasn't grieving for my wife. But now I'm not so sure about that. But having you here, it's... freed something in me. Sparked a flame. You... you—"

He stopped, a frown biting into his brow. Then he chuckled softly.

"I've never had a problem finding the correct words before, Fern. But now I feel at a loss to explain all that I'm feeling."

His voice was a warm rumble, like a low, primitive drumbeat that thudded through her being.

"You've forced me to experience many new

things,'' he admitted. ''You've made me face things I didn't want to look at.''

Fern became aware of something...some strange phenomenon. A touch on her skin. A prickle around her ankles and calves. It seemed as if something was growing right out of the ground, winding around her legs, curling and looping and securing. The sensation felt so tangible—so corporeal—that she actually glanced down at her feet. But she saw nothing.

When she gazed into Paul's dark eyes, the emotion in them had softened. His gaze seemed so deep she got the impression she could fall headlong into it. And she wouldn't mind doing it, either.

''I'm glad I met you,'' he whispered, leaning toward her. ''I'm glad you came to stay with Katy and me. I'm glad you helped us.'' His tone went rough. ''I'm glad you helped *me,* Fern. So very glad.''

She was hypnotized by those luscious eyes, that handsome face, that velvety voice. His thumb traced a semicircle on the sensitive underside of her wrist.

''It's as if I've been fumbling around in the dark—'' he inched closer ''—and you came into my life like a bright and glowing light, illuminating... everything.''

He placed his lips on hers, lightly, sweetly, the heat of him penetrating to her marrow. Her eyes rolled closed, and she inhaled the warm scent of him deep into her lungs. This contact, this exhilarating and intimate act of the kiss, was something she would never, in all her life, get enough of.

When Paul kissed her, she experienced a gnawing hunger, but that need soon changed...intensified. As he deepened the kiss, his tongue plundering her mouth, she was filled with something else. Some concentrated feeling that went beyond hunger, some powerful urge she couldn't identify—a sweet yet savage demand that was so new, so unfamiliar to her that she had no means of coping with it.

His hand slipped upward to cup her breast, the heat of him nearly scorched her through the fabric of her top. The profound need in her built until she thought she could no longer contain it.

"The secret," she murmured against his hot, moist lips. She pulled back to study his gaze. "Have y' changed your mind? Are y' willin' to show me?"

He pressed his nose against her temple, seeming to drink in the fragrance of her, and Fern was so captivated by the act that she feared she would melt away to nothingness.

"Ah, Fern, I tried to fight it. I did. With every fiber of my soul. I thought you'd be better off with someone else. Someone who could share the newness and the wonder of...your first time. But you've touched me. You've changed me. I can't let you go. Not now. Not ever."

That odd prickling sensation around her ankles moved upward, over her knees and thighs, entwining itself around her waist. It was so strong now that Fern frowned.

The smoky tendrils didn't feel soft and wispy any longer. They seemed to be growing stronger, colder, more solid, like...*chains.*

Fern's eyes flew open as panic straightened her spine. She flattened her palm firmly against Paul's rock-hard chest and pushed herself free of him. She stood up and physically moved away from the enchanting allure that threatened to ensnare her. Moved away from the invisible chains that had very nearly affixed her forever to this world...to this life.

"I don't belong here, Paul!" she said, emotion making her voice louder than she'd intended it to be. "I have to return to Sidhe. And I have to go right away!"

He looked bewildered. "But I thought you were in the States for an extended visit?" he asked. "I know we never talked about how long you'd stay, but I never thought you'd want to go home this soon." He sobered. "I don't want you to go. Katy needs you. I need you." His voice softened. "I want you."

The tendrils snaked their way toward her. She couldn't see them, but she sure felt them. They were coming for her. She had to do something. Fast!

Without pausing to think, she blurted, *"I'm a pixie, Paul! I don't belong in your world."*

As if the dullahan himself had paid a visit, the air—the very night—went as still as death. At first Paul looked confused. But then his gaze lit with a hesitant humor.

"Whatever you say, Tinkerbell," he quipped. He padded the seat beside him. "Come back over here and sit down. Let's kick up a little fairy dust."

Oh, by all that was holy! He thought she was joking.

Then common sense slammed into her like a well-aimed stone between the eyes. How could he think anything else? He wasn't a believer. The only fairy world he knew of was the one conjured by humans and labeled as folklore.

He would never understand. She'd never make him

believe her. What had she been thinking to blurt out the truth like that?

She hadn't thought. That was the problem.

Well, the course she'd set might not have been the wisest one, or the easiest one, but she was going to follow it just the same. Whether he let her go home because she'd been able to convince him of the truth, or because he thought she'd lost her bloomin' mind, it mattered not. The important thing was getting back to where she belonged.

"I'm not ribbin' you, Paul. I'm as serious as I can be. I'm a pixie. A fairy from Sidhe. I don't belong in your mortal world." She rested her fist on her hip. "I let you believe that Sidhe was the name of a town. But it's not. It's a...it's a place. A realm. The Gray Lands. The Fay World. Fairyland. It's an enchanted world filled with magical creatures. Silkies and dwarves and brownies and a host of others too numerous to name."

His grin never faltered during her explanation. "Okay," he said, drawing out the word in a way that clearly expressed his disbelief. "Prove it."

It was all she could do not to stamp her foot in frustration. "I can't. For one thing, I can't metamorphose where the human eye can witness—"

"I'll be happy to close my eyes," he injected.

"Paul! Even if I could change right here and right now, you wouldn't see me. Nonbelievers are blind to fairy folk."

"How convenient."

She fumed silently, doing all she could to keep her annoyance at bay. "Look, y' don't have to believe me, but y' don't have to belittle me, either."

That knocked the smile off his face. "You're serious."

Fern just looked at him.

His brows arched high. "You honestly expect me to believe that ridiculous story? I've heard some strange things in my day, Fern, but even you have to admit...this is truly bizarre."

There was a hesitation in his tone, his body language. She knew he was expecting her to come clean at any moment, to laugh and tell him she was only teasing him. But she had no intention of doing that. She was telling him the truth. If he couldn't handle it, that was his problem.

Then her heart was overcome with a mournful sensation. She cocked her head as if she was listening. But the desolation wasn't audible. She couldn't hear it, couldn't see it. But she felt it, nonetheless.

"Oh, Paul—" tears sprang to Fern's eyes "—I need to help her."

Concern clouded his dark eyes. "Help who? Katy? I didn't hear her call out."

Fern shook her head. "Not Katy. Another pixie. A fairy just like me. Well, not just like me. She's in her pixie form. She's lost. She could be hurt. She needs my help."

"What are you talking about?"

He actually looked worried now.

"There's a pixie in Central Park. When you took me there for the picnic that day, I...I couldn't see her. She was hiding from me in the trees...but I *felt* her. I heard her crying. Can you take me there?"

"You want to go to Central Park *now?* After dark?"

The expression she steadied on him made her feelings clear.

"Absolutely not," he said. "It's not safe." He shook his head as if he couldn't believe he was even discussing the issue. "Fern, this is craziness."

"I need to go to the park," she insisted.

He stood, held his hands up, palms outward. "Okay, okay. Let's just calm down here for a second." He approached her, took hold of her wrist. "I think I understand what's happening here. You're afraid. You told me before that you've never...that you're a virgin. Things were getting pretty hot and heavy between us just now. I can see why you might want to slow things down a little. But, Fern, honey, you don't have to make up outlandish stories in order to—"

She jerked her hand from his grasp. "I am not makin' up stories!"

Storm clouds brewed all around him, lightning flashed hotly in his eyes, thunder roared in his tone as he said, "Well, I damned sure don't believe that you're a pixie princess!"

Fern narrowed her gaze, her own anger flaring inside her like a white-hot poker, jabbing her until she could no longer control her tongue. "Ya foolish man! I never said a thing about being a princess. And to tell you the truth, you can take a flying leap off a toadstool because I don't care *what* you believe!"

She shoved her way past him on her way to the door.

Behind her he yelled, "I can't do that, now, can I?

In the mortal world, as you called it, toadstools don't come that big!''

Fern wouldn't have been surprised if steam had been rolling off the top of her head as he followed her into the house, she was that flamin' mad.

Chapter Nine

Turning herself into a pixie hadn't been hard at all. She suspected it was because she was absolutely, positively spitfire angry with Paul. He didn't have to believe her, but he shouldn't have ridiculed her.

Her worry over the Central Park pixie took precedence over everything else at the moment. That forlorn feeling that swept over her had been amazingly forceful. That poor pixie was beside herself for some reason, and Fern had every intention of finding out why. If Paul wouldn't help her get to the park in the city, Fern would get there on her own.

Slipping out her bedroom window, she shot skyward, high above the treetops, looked all around to get her bearings and then headed for the bright lights of the city. The glow was faraway, but she was determined to get there.

Hours later, after several rest stops, she found herself on the outskirts of New York City. Even at this time of night the city was a bustle of activity. Cars and trucks, buses and yellow taxicabs crowded the roadways. People were everywhere, coming and going along the grid-like sidewalks.

Fern soared high again and found the huge, dark rectangle she knew was the park. She could smell the fresh scent of the vegetation, grass, oaks, evergreens, flowering bushes. This was the park, all right. But it was bigger than she'd imagined. How would she find the pixie?

She listened intently, hoping to hear—or at least feel—the pixie's sadness. But Fern neither heard nor sensed a thing.

Flying in a straight line, she conducted her search in as logical a manner as possible. At one point she saw a soft glow, but her nose quickly told her it was no pixie. A boy hunkered over, sucking on a nasty cigarette, puffing vile smoke into the air. Fern continued her methodical sweep of the park.

Finally Fern caught sight of the pixie through the trees. Speeding up, Fern caught up with her.

"Hey," she called out.

The pixie was so startled by Fern's appearance that her wings stopped flapping, and she tumbled down into a wild tangle of yellow blooming forsythia branches. Alarmed, Fern hurried to help her climb out.

"Are you all right?" she asked.

With her long, flowing raven's-wing hair and her cobalt-blue eyes, the pixie was a vision of loveliness. Fern smiled cheerily. The pixie just stared for several long, silent moments.

Tentatively the pixie reached out and touched Fern.

"I'm as real as real can be," Fern assured her.

Her delicate features lifted with what could only be described as elation. Her fluttering wings raised her into the air, and she fairly attacked Fern with a hug. They embraced and spun happily in the air.

Once they parted and settled down on a nearby rock, Fern introduced herself.

"I'm Gillie," the pixie told her. "I'm so happy to see your face. It's hard to believe I'm not alone anymore."

"I'm sorry I didn't come sooner," Fern confessed.

"Sooner?" Gillie was clearly confused.

"I was in the park not too long ago. I had lunch. I heard you…crying."

"You did?" Gillie's bewilderment only deepened. "I didn't see you. I didn't…wait. I remember…one day I thought a human was calling out to me—" She stopped, her eyes going wide.

Fern nodded guiltily. "That was me. I've broken the rules, I know."

Gillie's shoulders rounded. "Don't worry. I won't tell a soul. Who would I tell stuck here in this place all by my lonesome? Besides that, I broke the rules, too. And I'm paying the price now."

"You made the change, too?" There was awe in Fern's voice. Knowing that another pixie had made the same mistake she had made her feel less alone. She guessed misery really did love company.

Nodding, Gillie offered a sad smile. "You did it for a human man, didn't you? I did, too. But at least we both came to our senses."

Remembering just how close she came to being tethered to the mortal world forever, Fern said, "At first I thought it was little Katy, the babe I'd taken a shine to, who had me turning into a human. I've always had a soft spot for little ones. But then I learned that it wasn't the child at all. It was her father. Paul is his name. He was the one who caused me to change.''

A frown creased Gillie's forehead. ''What do you mean, he *made* you change? You didn't turn human on your own?''

Fern lifted one shoulder. ''I didn't turn human consciously at first, if that's what you're asking. It was an accident that threw the three of us together. The babe reached out and grabbed hold of me just as her father was getting her ready to go out. I became trapped in the sleeve of Katy's sweater. I didn't get meself free until we were already on the airplane. But—'' she shook her head, remembering ''—I didn't intentionally turn human that first time…it just sort of happened when I was thinking about helping Paul with Katy.''

''Airplane? You came here on one of those big silvery contraptions in the sky?'' Gillie was evidently fixated on this part of Fern's story. ''I knew I wasn't in Sidhe any longer, but I had no idea where I was.''

Gillie's chin trembled suddenly, and Fern knew the pixie had been traumatized by her experience of feeling lost and all alone.

''How *did* you get here, Gillie?'' she asked softly, reaching out to gently brush a strand of the pixie's shiny black hair over her shoulder. ''Tell me what happened to you?''

''I've been in love with Kennon O'Brian for as long as I can remember,'' Gillie whispered. ''His hair is as red as the blazing sunset. And his eyes...ah, Fern, they're as blue and as deep as the sea, I tell y'." Anguish seemed to drape her like a heavy cloak. "He didn't even know I existed, me bein' a pixie and him bein' human and all. He started talkin' to one and all about going away to seek his fortune. He was goin' to leave Ireland. He was going to leave me! Without even thinking about it, I slipped into his suitcase the night he was packing to go. I didn't know where I'd end up, I only knew I wanted to be with him."

Fern's heart went out to Gillie.

"I thought I'd never survive the trip," Gillie continued. "I was in that suitcase forever. I was cold and hungry and cramped. I was jostled and tossed about, there was a great rumbling vibration and the racket 'bout split me eardrums, it did. I was scared outta me skin."

The description of Gillie's plane ride was what Fern remembered, too.

"But finally Kennon opened the case and I was free." She nibbled her lip, anxiety pinching her brow. "I'd always been taught it was wrong to turn human."

Fern nodded even though she knew Gillie wasn't paying attention. It was a rule drilled into the head of every pixie.

"It was love that had me takin' the risk, Fern. But even when I became a woman, Kennon still didn't notice me. I was crushed when..."

Poignant emotion made the rest of Gillie's thought fade into oblivion.

She sighed deeply. "You need to know, Fern, it isn't your Paul who enabled you to change. It's the feelings y' have for him. The stronger the feelings grow, the less control y'll have over your magic."

The pixies shared a moment of silent horror at the notion.

"I suspect," Gillie continued, softly, "that there might even come a time when the emotions could grow so strong that y'd lose your power to turn back into a pixie altogether."

The thing that activated her power to change had been in her? The question filled Fern with wonder. All along, it had been her *feelings* for Paul that allowed her to change, and not the man himself?

Fern thought about the chainlike tendrils that nearly shackled her to the mortal world tonight when she and Paul had kissed. It hadn't been Paul at all, but her growing feelings for him that had nearly imprisoned her. Was she in love with him? Trepidation knotted in her stomach.

Evidently sensing Fern's anxiety, Gillie asked, "How far did things go between the two of y'?" When her question was met with silence, Gillie pressed, "Y' haven't kissed him, have y'?"

After a moment's hesitation, Fern offered a single, fearful nod.

"Oh, my. Y' haven't voiced your feelings to him?"

"No. I haven't gone that far."

Then Gillie asked, "Do you love him, Fern?"

She was too afraid to answer. Instead she pointed out, "You said you loved Kennon, but you were able to change."

"He scorned me," she answered. "I was furious with him. And I left."

Fern remembered how easy it was for her to become a pixie tonight after Paul had refused to believe her.

"I had no idea where I was," Gillie told her, "but that hadn't mattered at the time. I just flew. And I found this place. It was so nice and green."

The sadness suddenly engulfing Gillie emanated from her in strong concentric circles, and Fern felt it.

Gillie's head dipped. "But it's not Sidhe. That much I know. It's not even Ireland. The humans talk with all manner of dialects here. I've been all over this patch of forest and there's not a single fairy to be found."

"You're in America," Fern told her.

The other pixie's mouth rounded. Amazement had her voice softening. "I was carried across the great sea?" She heaved a sigh. "How will I ever get back home?"

"Don't you worry." Fern mustered up a smile meant to offer Gillie hope. "I'm going to help you. I'll get us both back to Sidhe, safe and sound. Of that you can be sure."

Paul stroked his fingers over Fern's shoulder, down her arm, over her hand where it rested at her side. His tender touch continued over the curve of her bare hip and thigh. Fern sighed in ecstasy and rolled onto her back. He loomed over her, pressed his mouth to her neck, feathering hot, languid kisses down the full length of her throat. She tipped up her chin to surrender full access to him. His head slowly dipped lower, his sweet breath tickling her skin, and when he took her dusky, taut nipple ever so gently between his teeth, she moaned out her need, fire igniting at the very core of her.

The tugging on her foot was odd and out of sync with what she was experiencing. Something prickly and warm nudged against her ankle and had her swimming reluctantly and groggily from the haze of sleep. Her lids felt weighted and she struggled to open her eyes. She swiped the back of her hand across her forehead to push the thatch of hair from her face. She moistened her dry lips, and then a startled yelp ripped from her throat when she saw—

A *horse?*

The magnificent beast nuzzled the curled toe of her silk slipper, its hot breath blowing over her ankle when it snorted nervously. She jerked her foot out of harm's way and sat up on the mossy ground. Sudden fright had her spine straightening, her leg muscles bunching to flee. Early-morning sunlight glared, and she raised her hand to protect her eyes. That was when she saw him—the big, burly police officer sitting astride the horse.

"It isn't safe for you to be sleeping in the park," the man said, warning clear in his firm tone. "It's also against the law."

Unable to shake the befuddlement holding her captive, Fern took several seconds to realize that he saw her—that he was speaking to her! She was human. That touchy-feely dream she'd had of Paul had stirred her emotions to the point that she'd transformed.

Last night she and Gillie had talked and talked until both of them were yawning. Fern had been walloped by fatigue after her long flight from Paul's house to

Central Park. Gillie had invited her to curl up on the soft moss at the base of a tree.

Thoughts of Gillie had Fern looking all around her, but the pixie was nowhere in sight. Fern got the distinct feeling that that fact should be worrisome, but she didn't have time to ponder it for long.

"Are you okay?" the officer asked. "You seem a little confused."

"No." Fern shook her head vehemently. "Thank y' kindly, but I'm fine."

"You're not from around here." It wasn't a question. "Are you visiting someone? Are you lost? What's your name?"

"I appreciate your concern." The hail of what should have seemed simple questions filled her with panic, and that was what finally cleared the morning fog from Fern's brain. "But truly I'll be just fine."

She made the bold proclamation even though she knew good and well that, as a human, she had no means of getting herself back to Paul's house. No money, no directions, nothing. Ah well, she'd think of something. She pushed herself up from the ground, swiped at the blades of grass and wrinkles scattered across the front of her dress.

The man dismounted. "I'm not so sure of that, miss. I'm afraid I'm going to have to ask that you let me help you."

"I'm okay—"

His fingers slid firmly around her upper arm. "I think I'm going to have to insist."

"Gillie," she said, sudden dread lumping in her stomach, "I think I may be in a spot of trouble. Stay with me."

"I'll stay right with you, miss," the officer replied. "Have no fear. But my name's not Gillie. It's Max. I'm Officer Max Harrison. Let's head over to the station and see if we can straighten things out for you."

Not too long afterward, Fern found herself sitting on a hard, narrow bench in the police station. There was a rough-looking man handcuffed to an adjacent bench not too far away. The stench of stale beer wafting off him was overpowering. He kept grinning at Fern, and once he even winked a scarlet, watery eye at her, but she made a valiant attempt to ignore him.

Officers milled about, many of them sipping cups of fragrant coffee, munching a breakfast of Danishes or doughnuts.

She'd looked around for a place to slip off to, a place where no one could see her. If she became a pixie, she could fly off with no fear of being seen. Surely she could find Paul's house. Pixies were known for their wonderful sense of direction.

"Officer Harrison?" she called. "May I use the ladies' room?"

He pointed in the direction, and she made a beeline down the hallway.

She closed herself in the cubicle and focused. Several long moments passed. It seemed that no amount of concentration enabled a successful metamorphosis. There was too much noise and commotion going on at the station house, she decided.

A firm knock on the door made Fern jump.

"You okay in there?" Officer Harrison called through the door.

"I'll be right out," she answered. With a sigh of frustration, Fern realized she'd have to give up the effort altogether. It seemed that escaping the situation would be impossible.

But before leaving the restroom, Fern whispered, "Gillie? Are y' there?"

She couldn't actually see her pixie friend—and again that fact bothered her mightily. She was a believer, wasn't she? But she was aware of a glimmering light in the periphery of her vision, and something in her, intuition or simple fairy awareness, told her that Gillie was nearby.

"I'll get us out of this yet," Fern assured her. "I promise you that."

When she exited the room, the officer was waiting in the hallway.

"Okay," he said, "you've put me off long enough. It's time to answer some questions."

Fern offered him a resigned nod, and then followed him to his desk. She confessed that she was just visiting America, that she was from Ireland, and then she'd given the officer Paul's name and explained that she worked as a nanny taking care of his daughter. However, when she was asked for his exact address and phone number, and wasn't able to supply either, the officer shot her a doubtful look.

"Well, I wouldn't know the number now, would I?" she quipped. "Why would I be wantin' to call the house when I'm livin' there?" She plunked a balled fist on her hip. "And I haven't been staying there long enough to memorize the address."

The excuse sounded plausible enough to her.

Paul's telephone number was unlisted, but luckily one of the employees at the barracks produced a copy of Paul's novel from her desk drawer. Officer Harrison had to call the publisher several times before someone answered the phone at this early hour. Evidently reluctant to give out Paul's home telephone number, the secretary who answered agreed to supply the contact information of Paul's agent. Harrison hung up with a sigh, only to punch in the numbers for yet another call.

Finally he replaced the receiver in its cradle. "Well—" he directed his gaze at Fern "—now we wait. Paul Roland's agent has no idea if he hired a nanny. But he said he'd call your employer and check it out. If you're legit, then I'm sure someone will show up before too long."

"Oh, Paul will come fer me." Of that Fern was certain. "But I'm sure not lookin' forward to it. Not one little bit."

Paul gripped the steering wheel with both hands, his brain churning, his ire roiling as he drove down the interstate. How the hell had Fern gotten herself into the city? He hadn't even realized she'd gone. Hadn't heard her leave the house this morning. And his agent had informed him that Fern had been carrying no purse and no ID when she'd been picked up. Had she lost her glorious, redheaded mind?

An Irish pixie, indeed! How could Fern expect anyone to believe that outlandish story?

She'd become frightened, that's what had happened. He'd gotten a little too aggressive with his affections last night. He'd overwhelmed her. She was innocent. He should have remembered that. She was unknowing of the ways of intimate relations. Fear—

plain and simple—was why she'd blurted out that astonishing and bizarre tale.

I don't belong here. Her words floated through his brain.

I only came to help.

Memories swam and darted around in his head like a school of tiny, colorful fish.

He thought about the first time he'd seen Fern. He'd looked up from where he sat struggling with Katy and had seen a beautiful and serene woman wearing that simple flowing dress, those slippers she wore with the odd up-turned toes. There had been a glow about her...a radiance that he remembered noticing even after all this time.

And she *had* shown up just when he'd needed help with Katy on the plane. Nothing he'd been able to do had calmed his fussy daughter. Yet with Fern's coddling, Katy had settled right down. In fact, Katy had greeted Fern with a peculiar familiarity, had gone right to her. His clingy little girl—who was normally fearful of people she didn't know—had actually fallen asleep in the arms of a stranger.

He remembered thinking how odd it had seemed. But he'd been so relieved to have Fern's help, he hadn't given the matter the thought it deserved.

Paul let his thoughts roll backward in time. He couldn't remember having seen her at the gate before he'd boarded the plane, now that he took the time to think about it. And she was beautiful with her creamy skin, her delicate features, those wild, burnished curls and those arresting aqua eyes. He'd been preoccupied with Katy, of course, but he *was* a red-blooded man...he couldn't imagine not noticing a woman as striking as Fern had she been part of the boarding passengers that day at the airport.

"Oh, no," he muttered out loud in the car, "I cannot believe I'm even considering this crazy idea."

"Cwazy!" Katy clapped her hands gleefully.

Paul looked in the rearview mirror at his daughter who was securely strapped in her car seat in the back.

"That's exactly what it is, Katy," he agreed whole-heartedly with a firm nod. "Crazy."

He had to drive around the block several times before he found an available parking space near the police station. Then he got Katy out of the car.

"Come on, sweetie," he said, settling her on his hip. "Let's go find Fern."

Katy's dark eyes lit with excitement.

Inside, he zeroed in on Fern almost immediately, and he was bombarded with emotion. Relief swept though him to see that she was truly okay. But he was also peeved to no end to know she'd left the house this morning without telling him about her plans.

He introduced himself to Officer Harrison and shook the man's hand. When asked if Fern worked for him, he answered in the affirmative and explained that she really was Katy's nanny. He turned to her.

"I'd have brought you to the park, Fern," he said to her. "All you had to do was ask."

"I did ask," she pointed out stiffly. "You said no."

"I said no last night," he reminded her. "And I gave you a perfectly good explanation, too."

"When I woke her up this morning, sir," the officer said, "I did tell her that it wasn't safe for her to be spending the night in the park."

"Spending the night? But..." Paul couldn't believe his ears. He worked to put his disjointed thoughts together. *"You slept in Central Park?"*

The volume of his voice attracted the attention of curious onlookers, but it only seemed to antagonize Fern. Her shoulders squared, her mouth pursed tightly and she crossed her arms over her chest.

"When exactly did you leave the house?" he asked accusingly. "And how on earth did you get yourself into the city?"

Her perfectly arched brows rose a fraction. "I already explained to you that I'm a pixie." With slow and precise enunciation, she added, "I flew."

Paul blinked, heat rushing to his face. He darted a quick glance at the officer, who seemed to be in a quandary trying to decide if he should be concerned over Fern's answer or if he should chuckle at what he obviously hoped was a comic act of some kind.

The policeman directed his gaze at Paul and murmured, "She has shown some signs of confusion."

Fern turned her ire on the officer then. "I'll have you know I am not the least confused!"

Ignoring her outburst, the officer said to Paul, "She called me Gillie earlier."

"It wasn't you I was talkin' to when I said that, y' big brute!" Her chin jutted out defensively. To Paul she snapped, "I told you about the other pixie. The pixie in the park I needed to look for. That's why I had to come to the city. Well, I found her, and her name's Gillie."

The officer shook his head, frowning at Paul. "She was alone when I picked her up, Mr. Roland. There was no Gillie around."

"Of course you couldn't see her, you nitwit! You're *human!*"

The cop shot her a pointed look then, but he did an excellent job of remaining composed. "Yes, and I'm trying to be a concerned human right now, miss. That'll be enough name calling, if you don't mind."

Fearing that reprisal wasn't too far away in Fern's future, Paul calmly suggested, "Fern, let's talk about all this when we get home." He asked the officer, "Is there any reason you need to hold her? Are you planning to press loitering charges against her or anything? Or can I take her home now?"

He realized his speech pattern had accelerated, that he was shooting questions at the policeman like bullets from an automatic weapon. He was only reacting to the sudden urge to get Fern out of the police station before she caused more problems than he could fix.

"No," Officer Harrison said, "I have no reason to hold her. At first I thought she might be a...well, a professional woman, if you know what I mean. But she didn't fit the pattern. Then I feared she was a runaway. A kid who needed help. But once I got a good look at her—" he danced around the words "—I could see she was a full-grown adult. But then she started talking—"

So that was her downfall, Paul mused darkly.

"—and, like I said, she seemed a little out of it," the officer continued. "So I brought her to the station."

"I appreciate your help," Paul said. "Thank you so much for tracking me down. I know it was time-consuming, and you probably had other pressing things to take care of."

"Well, now you're makin' me feel guilty for having taken up the man's precious time," Fern muttered. "I told him I was fine, that I didn't need his flamin' help."

Paul sent her a look. "You need to be quiet. We're leaving. We'll talk about all this at home."

Sudden stubbornness radiated from her. "I'm not at all sure I want to go with you now."

He just looked at her, giving her time to mull over her choices, which he knew were few, at best.

Exhaling in a huff, she lowered her balled fists to her sides and headed for the door. After a final nod at the officer, Paul followed after her.

He didn't trust himself to speak until they'd left the city behind. As he steered the car off the exit ramp that spilled out onto the road leading to the suburbs, he said, "Fern, I hope you realize how dangerous your behavior was. The city is full of thieves and thugs. People who wouldn't bat an eye over hurting you."

"How many times must I tell you? I was never in harm's way. I was a pixie when I left the house last night. Humans can't hurt us. Nonbelievers can't even see us."

His teeth ground until a pinpoint of pain shot through his tense jaw muscle. How long did she intend to keep up this farce?

She gazed out the window, her tone softening as she added, "But I am concerned. I had thought believers *could* see us fairy folk. Being a pixie makes me more than a believer, I would say, yet when I'm human I can't see Gillie. I sense her. And I can almost see her glow. But I can't actually see her."

Aggravation got the better of him and he scoffed, "So this Gillie is here, is she? She's in the car with us?"

"Of course she is, Paul," Fern answered. "She's keeping Katy company."

It wasn't until that moment that he became cognizant of it—Katy's laughter. She giggled and chattered as if she were playing with a newfound friend. And he realized that she'd been doing it ever since they got into the car back in the city.

A dark cloud formed over his head. "This is the biggest bunch of hogwash I have ever heard. I'm not going to discuss this silliness, Fern."

He clamped his mouth shut, intending to say not another word on the subject. In the back seat, his daughter continued to laugh and babble in utter delight.

Chapter Ten

"Are you still too angry to talk to me?" Fern asked Paul from where she stood in the doorway of Katy's room.

He sat in the rocking chair, cradling his slumbering daughter. The two of them made an endearing sight. Even though it was a normal nap time for Katy, Fern almost felt she was intruding on a special father-and-daughter time; however, Fern had waited for Paul to approach her all morning and he hadn't. She felt compelled to seek him out.

"I'm not angry, Fern," he said. "Come on in. We can talk in here. I know I should put Katy in her crib, but if we're quiet we won't disturb her. She's sound asleep, and she looks so sweet I just want to hold her a while longer." He pressed a butterfly kiss to Katy's downy hair. "She's growing up too fast. You helped me to see that. I want to savor every moment I have with her."

When his dark eyes locked onto Fern's as she approached him, she was captivated by the sheer intensity of him. Her steps slowed and then stopped altogether.

"I want to savor every moment I have with you, too, Fern," he said. "It looks like you're determined to leave me soon."

His tone was whispery, but it couldn't have affected her more had he shouted the words at her. Suddenly all the oxygen in the room seemed to have evaporated and her knees felt wobbly. Without even thinking about it, she sank to the floor and sat on the plush carpeting just a few feet from where he reclined in the rocker.

"I don't want the time we have left to be ruined with anger or bad feelings." He paused a moment to take a slow, deep breath, and she couldn't help but be aware of the fact that his heart was heavy. "I had hoped you would stay, but you've made it clear you want to go back to Ireland."

He moistened his lips, and the memory of his delicious kisses—both real and imagined—flashed into her thoughts. Her own heart took on a heaviness that was both grave and poignant.

Regret tightened his features. "I'm sorry if I frightened you last night. I'm sorry if I pushed too hard or came on too strong. I sure didn't mean to make you go to such extremes to...to let me know you wanted no part of me."

"Oh, but—" She felt spellbound, and her answer came without an inkling of thought or self-consciousness. "I *did*. I *do*."

"Then why the strange story?" The question

wasn't accompanied by irritation or anger. No, instead he looked unmistakably baffled. "Why do you want to go back to Ireland?"

Oh, how she wanted to stay! But she couldn't. She just couldn't.

"I *have* to go back, Paul," she said. "Y' have to understand that much."

His dark head shook from side to side. "I don't understand, Fern. I tried to tell you how I feel. I tried to explain it to you. But it only made you go off the deep end, coming up with that wild craziness. It was entertaining, yes, but you have to admit it was outrageous. And then you ran off to Central Park all by yourself. And I still haven't a clue how you got yourself there." He paused, seeming to quell a shiver. "When I think of the danger you could have faced."

She wanted to reach out to him, but she dared not. Her grasp on her fairy powers was tentative. She could sense it. Any physical contact with Paul, she feared, would cause her to lose her ability to metamorphose. "I'm sorry y' were worried. I truly am. But Gillie needed—"

His breath left him in a sharp rush, cutting her sentence off. Then he smiled ruefully. "You really think that pixie tale is going to change how I feel about you? It's not. I wouldn't care if you tried to entice me to believe you were a mermaid or a troll. I still need you to know that I—"

"Paul—" the need to stop him welled up so strongly that she had to act on it "—don't say any more. Please. It's not safe. For me, I mean. It's the emotions, y' see. They're a danger to me. They've got me very near to losing me powers, as it is. I can not have you confessing any more.''

He just pressed his lips together and fell silent.

Awkwardness settled in. In an attempt to banish it, Fern offered him a small grin and quipped, ''Where I come from, sea nymphs are called silkies, and although the salty ocean is peaceful, I'm not fond enough of the water to spend my life diving through the waves. And trolls? Why, they're covered with warts from head to foot and live in damp, dark places.'' Her nose wrinkled with distaste. ''I like being a pixie, Paul. I do. It's a joyful, carefree existence. And we live forever.'' Sheepishness had her head tilting a fraction. ''Well, if not forever, then at least for hundreds and hundreds of years.''

The glowering expression that made his chin dip had her crooning, ''Now, now. I know y' don't believe a word that's coming out of my mouth. And I wish there was some way I could convince you.''

She brightened, her spine straightening. ''I knew Maire when she was a babe, Paul. I played with her just as I played with Katy when the two of y' visited Ireland.''

''Fern, don't.''

''No, really,'' she insisted. She had to find some way to persuade him she was telling him the truth. ''I can tell y' about her. She was a lovely babe. Of the black Irish she was. Her skin was fair like most everyone on the Emerald Isle, but her hair was black and shiny as the finest polished onyx. Thick and straight.''

Closing her eyes, Fern thought back over the years. Of the time she'd spent with Maire.

"Her eyes were blue as the summer sky," Fern continued. "Sparkling with curiosity and excitement, quick wit and intelligence. How she loved to laugh. She was so creative!" Fern's eyes went round, her smile widening as she remembered. "She loved to sing. And dance. When she was just a tot, she entertained everyone in the village with songs she made up herself, with dances she invented. Did y' know she used to write her own poetry books? And they were complete with beautiful illustrations. Those books were somethin' she kept hidden, even from her own ma. She hid them away in the back of her closet, she did. And she did all of these things before she had time to question the reality of fairy creatures."

Paul had gone utterly still.

"Children can see us," Fern said quietly. "Maire saw me. She saw my friends, too. Usually, children grow up and lose their belief. They listen too intently to the adults around them who insist we're nothing but myth. Children stop believing in magic, stop trusting that there really is a fairy world. Usually. But Maire didn't forget. The memory might have grown dim in her mind, but it was there just the same. Where do you think this came from?"

Fern spread her arms wide, indicating the roomsize mural Maire had hand-painted for her baby daughter.

Pointing at one particular pixie on the wall, Fern said, "Right there is the proof that Maire never forgot me. Just as I never forgot her. She painted me on that wall. And she sketched me in her book. The memories we made together were strong in her. Just as strong as they are in me. Those memories drew me

back to the nursery when Katy was visiting Ireland.
I guess you could say, Paul, that in a roundabout way
Maire brought me to Katy. She brought me to you.
It's because of her—because of her belief in me, I
guess you could say—that I was able to be near to
help you when you needed me.''

Paul's silent gaze swept to the mural, his attention
riveted to the mystical creature Fern had pointed to.

Sudden relief allowed her muscles to ease. Peace
draped itself over her like a warm shawl. She'd explained the best way she knew how, offered him what
proof she could. She could do no more than that.

The corners of her mouth curled. ''It's okay if y'
don't believe. You're a human. An adult human.
You're not meant to believe, y' see. Actually, it's the
disbelief of humans that protects us fairies. All that's
important to me, really, is that y' understand that,
even though I might not *want* to go back, I *need* to
go back. It's where I belong.''

Paul was silent for a long time. He sat there just
looking at her. His dark gaze was reflective, intense,
and she couldn't begin to read his expression.

Finally he murmured, ''If you need to go home to
Sidhe, I'll see that you get there.''

A light summer breeze fluffed the sheer curtains
hanging at the nursery window. Paul gently laid his
daughter on the crib mattress, covered her with a cool,
cotton sheet and then straightened. His little girl was
a treasure, he thought, staring down at her. Her
breathing was whispery and even.

Fern had left him alone with Katy just a few
minutes ago after he'd promised to search the Internet

for information on the next airline flight bound for Ireland. He'd also promised to get Fern to the airport in time for the flight.

He was barely aware of the birds singing outside in the trees, hardly noticed the vibrant sunshine pouring into the room as his mind churned with what seemed a thousand thoughts at once.

Lifting his gaze to the pixie painted on the wall, the one with the curls of burnished copper, the one that Maire had positioned to overlook the crib of their beloved daughter, Paul mulled over all the things that Fern had told him.

How could Fern have known those things about Maire? Of course, the accurate physical description could have come from photos around the house. However, Fern had described Maire's character to a T. There had been a childlike essence about his deceased wife that even adulthood hadn't succeeded in quashing.

On this last trip to Ireland, Maire's parents had overcome their grief to the point that they'd actually enjoyed reminiscing about their daughter to Paul. They had told him that Maire was known around their village as "the little ray of sunshine" because she made people smile. With her made-up songs. And her made-up dances.

He hadn't known about Maire's childhood antics until his in-laws had told him about them. But he did know about Maire's talent for writing poetry. And he was aware that her gift had shown itself very early in her life.

With sure, measured steps, Paul left the nursery. The box full of Maire's memorabilia was calling out to him. He'd never once thought to get rid of it, knowing that someday Katy would appreciate this cherished prize that had once belonged to the mother she'd never had the opportunity to know.

He paused in the hallway and listened. The quiet house felt empty. He wondered where Fern might be.

The door of the attic opened with a creak. He carefully made his way up the narrow stairway. The summer heat had the room sweltering, and dust lay thick on the abandoned furniture pieces and storage trunks. He went to the shelf and took down the cedar box. He unfastened the latch. The clean, sharp scent of the wood billowed, cutting through the dry, dreary smell of disuse that settled all around him.

He flipped through the items from Maire's childhood: various photos, a yo-yo, a treasured birthday card, a diary...and at the bottom he found what he was looking for. The handmade book of poetry.

Paul pulled the delicate cardboard volume from the box and then slid the box back onto the shelf. He smiled down at the flowers drawn on the cover. They might have been sketched by a child, but the details in the colorful, droopy petals, in the veining of the leaves, showed that the artist had great potential.

Carefully he opened to the middle of the book and read a long, elaborate ode written in praise of nature and all it had to offer. Yes, his Maire had loved to write poetry. She'd used verse and rhyme to communicate her thoughts on all kinds of subjects. As a child, she'd created her very own books. And she'd kept these books a secret from everyone. Her very own secret treasure, she'd called them when she'd shared the story with Paul after they were married.

Yet Fern knew.

A flicker at the very fringes of his vision caught his attention. But when he looked up, he saw nothing out of the ordinary. His muscles tensed as he scanned every nook and cranny of the attic. All he saw were dust and shadows. He sighed, finally, and looked back at Maire's childhood book of poetry.

Then he saw it again, or thought he did, anyway. But every time he attempted to capture the light in his gaze, it seemed to disappear from his sight altogether. He forced himself to relax, and stared at the floor, every nerve ending in his body alert and vigilant.

That's when he saw it. A chip of chiseled crystal spinning in the sunlight, refracting pinpoints of pulsating color.

Logic and reason poked and prodded him, but he held them at bay. Before he could give it much thought at all, he whispered, "Fern?"

Addressing the vibrant energy filled him with a hope that warmed him from his scalp to the soles of his feet. He smiled.

"Fern," he said, louder this time. "I believe."

The airport was alive with activity. People were bustling down the corridors or anxiously standing in line at the check-in counters of the various airlines. A set of infant twins squalled their discontent while their older brother occupied himself by latching and unlatching the cords connecting the stanchions. Kinetic energy snapped and sparked in the air, and Fern supposed it was generated by the excitement of the travelers who were bound for or arriving from all those faraway locales.

True to his word, Paul had logged onto the Internet and discovered when the next flight for Ireland would be departing. After her encounter in the attic with Paul, Fern had decided to turn human and go for a walk across the meadows out in back of his home. Gillie had argued against what she warned was a dangerous adventure. But Fern had only laughed. Pixies couldn't resist any adventure, dangerous or not. Besides, Fern had been following her heart for a while now, and going against her deep-seated desire to experience the mortal world one last time had been impossible.

She'd reveled in the feel of the sun-warmed grass beneath her bare feet...she'd welcomed the weightiness of gravity on her human body...she'd longed for the summer breeze to blow across her skin. Underneath every square inch of her flesh, where millions of nerve endings that tingled and heated and glowed at the mere thought of being touched—by Paul.

If she'd sighed heavily once during that fateful walk, she'd sighed several dozen times.

Paul had ignited a mysterious fire in her that she'd never even known existed. He'd made her feel things...strange and delicious yearnings.

His touch. His kiss. Just thinking about them— about him—had made her heart ache. There were secrets that remained hidden from her even after weeks of being human. And they were secrets that she could only discover if she remained human.

It was in that instant that she'd realized...

She had a choice!

The realization had been accompanied by a barrage of excitement and fear and doubt and possibility. She'd wanted nothing more than to race home to Paul, to talk to him about the idea, to explore with him all her options.

However, once she'd arrived home and sought him out, she'd witnessed something new, something different in his expression, something that dimmed her enthusiasm to talk to him about her revelation, something that actually had her feeling quite…freakish. When he looked at her, she saw an odd mixture of wonder and, yes, fear in his eyes.

Self-consciousness had sprouted and taken root, its vines choking off both speech and the buoyant zest that had been bubbling inside her. She'd grown quiet, and had remained that way during the drive to the airport. Paul, too, had made the trip in silence. Katy giggled with Gillie in the back seat.

"There's the flight number," Paul said, stopping to peruse the wall of screens that televised the lists of incoming and departing flights. "Gate 7A. And the flight is on time." He glanced at his watch. "You a-and—" his tongue tripped charmingly "—Gillie don't have much time to spare."

Her insides were a riot of emotion. She turned to him and found that she was unable to smile. "We should say our goodbyes."

Reluctance rounded his shoulders as he shifted Katy into the crook of his opposite arm. Gillie had been doing an excellent job of entertaining the child since they'd gotten into the car to make the journey to the airport.

It seemed to Fern that Paul wanted to say something. She wished he would. Anything would be better than this nerve-racking silence.

Finally she could stand it no longer. "I want y' ta know," she said to him, "that I've enjoyed meself. I'm sure there will be some kinda backlash. I'll have someone to answer to for playin' so fast and loose with the rules." She offered him a rueful smile. "But bein' ostracized for a bit won't be all that bad, I guess. And it'll have been worth it to have had this chance to be—" words snagged in her throat, but she forced them out "—with you." Her face flushed and she softly added, "And with Katy, too, of course."

He searched her face, something unreadable shadowing his gaze. Anguish. Desperation. Fern couldn't say exactly what it was that constricted his handsome features so.

Finally, he blurted out, "I don't want to say goodbye, Fern. I've experienced enough loss. Enough grief. I don't want to hurt anymore. I don't want to miss you." He pressed his lips together and shook his head. "I'm not expressing myself very well at all."

Pain had his eyes glittering with moisture. "Imagine that—" emotion ripped and tore at his tone "—a man who earns his living with words unable to articulate his thoughts. But you've done that to me from the beginning, Fern. You've tipped my whole world upside down."

Her tummy quivered with sudden reserve. "It's been a bad thing, my bein' here?"

His breath left him in a rush. "How can you ask that?" He shook his head. "No. Not at all. Having you here hasn't been a bad thing. It's been a joy." A single tear welled up and trailed down his face, un-heeded. "A joy that I wish would never end."

Elation flashed through her like a bolt from a stormy sky. He didn't want this joy to end...and nei-ther did she!

Staying here with Paul and Katy was what she wanted more than anything, she realized. She wanted to be with them more than she wanted to be in her enchanted, carefree universe. More than whizzing across the lush, green hills and dales of Sidhe. More than her forever fairy existence. More than her mass of pixie friends.

And if she wanted it, why couldn't she have it? Hadn't she already decided that she had a choice in the matter?

Being here—being human—had given her a pur-pose that filled her with a deep satisfaction, a com-pleteness that she'd never experienced in her frivolous fairy world.

Fern loved Paul with every ounce of her being, and she desired to be with him, even if that meant surren-dering her immortality. It mattered not if they would have one year together or fifty. All she wanted was to spend the rest of her forever, however long that might be, with him.

Her decision made her positively jittery inside. She turned to Paul, intending to tell him all that was in her heart, but before she could say a word, she heard the flight number of the plane headed for Ireland be-ing announced over the intercom system.

She blinked. "We really do need to say our good-byes!"

Paul's fingers slid over her cheek. "Goodbye, my sweet Fern."

Her eyes rounded, and she reached up to take his hand in hers. "Not to me," she told him. "To Gillie. She needs to get on that airplane before it flies off without her."

Delight curled Paul's sexy mouth. "You're staying?"

She grinned. "The dullahan himself couldn't get me to leave you, now that I know you want me ta stay."

He put his arm around her and hugged her to him. "I do want you to stay. I do."

Warmth pulsated through her. "When we were in the attic and you professed your belief, I thought me heart would melt in me chest, Paul. It was a courageous thing, admitting something so crazy."

He chuckled. "It wasn't so courageous. I was all alone. Or nearly so, anyway. No one heard me but you."

"Oh, but you're wrong there," she told him. "Fate heard. Providence. The universe at large heard every word y' uttered. Y' can't ever take it back now."

"I wouldn't want to."

After a moment she admitted, "I was so scared. After you declared your belief y' looked at me differently. There was something in your eyes. Something that had me thinking you felt I was some kind of aberration."

He quickly shook his head. "That sounds so negative. That wasn't what I've been feeling at all." He paused, seeming to gather his thoughts. "First of all," he said, "it was an amazing idea to try to wrap my mind around. But once I did, I was overwhelmed by the...sheer magic of it.''

Pleasure curled in her belly.

"It's just as you said,'' he continued, ''when we're children, we're charmed by fairy tales, enthralled by a magician's sleight-of-hand. But as we grow, we're told that those things aren't real. That there is no magic...until all our enchantment is lost. But you've made me see that it's been there all along. Fairy tales *are* real. And happy endings do come true.'' He kissed the tip of her nose. ''All that matters is that this fairy tale just might be headed toward a happy ending.''

Then worry niggled at him. ''But what about that carefree existence you told me about. Humans don't live forever, Fern. To remain mortal means you'll be giving up so much. Maybe too much—''

Gently she reached up and pressed her fingers against his lips, hushing him. ''I'm happy to surrender every beautiful and blessed thing the fairy world has to offer,'' she told him. ''Even for just one more day with you.''

Gratitude and honor glistened in his dark gaze. ''I love you, Fern.''

He bent to kiss her, but not before she whispered against his mouth, ''And I love you, Paul. I'll love y' till the end of time.''

His lips were sweet and urgent against hers, a silent promise of things to come, of luscious secrets yet to be revealed.

A pleasant voice spoke over the loudspeaker, announcing the last call for all passengers heading to Ireland on the flight leaving from Gate 7A.

Fern broke off the kiss with a gasp. "Gillie!" She looked around her. "Y' must go now, Gillie," Fern said. "Tell everyone in Sidhe I said hello. I don't want y' worrin' about me. I'll be just fine." Hugging Paul around the waist as proof, she said, "I really am where I belong."

Epilogue

Fern sat on the deep window seat, staring out into the thick mist that covered the rolling Irish country-side. She never would have believed that such happiness and contentment were in her future.

Her days as a pixie had been filled with fun and frivolity. She'd certainly enjoyed it while it had lasted. But her life now seemed more worthwhile. More meaningful.

Love, she was learning, was an amazing emotion. It offered so much. The more of it that was given away, the more of it returned. It was magic. Pure, sweet magic!

Loving Paul and wee Katy, Fern felt, was something she was created to do. And knowing he loved her, knowing he was devoted to her happiness and well-being made her feel…well, she was still trying to find the perfect words to describe the beauty of all that she felt.

She and Paul had been married in a simple ceremony in Ireland just two short months after they'd
put Gillie on the plane. They'd had to dance around
the truth a bit to explain her lack of proper documents. The government employee had looked at Fern
askance, but the elderly woman had been a romantic
and had seen how much in love Fern and Paul were.
She'd signed the documents that enabled the vicar to
pronounce the vows that made them husband and
wife.

Katy had attended, of course, and Maire's parents
had graciously agreed to act as their witnesses. They
seemed to take a shining to Fern from the first moment they met. They were pleased that Paul had married a nice Irish girl.

Ireland was the perfect setting for their marriage
ceremony. Paul and Fern had traveled north into the
hill country to enjoy a few days alone on their hon-
eymoon. Katy was enjoying a visit with her grandparents.

Fern bent her knees, wrapping her arms around her
shins as she gazed out the window. Her smile was
never very far away these days, and it was quick to
play around the corners of her mouth ever since Paul
had first professed his love. All she had to do was
think of him, and her heart sang.

Night had fallen. Bedtime was looming. It was her
favorite time of day.

In the night…in the dark…under the cool sheets of
their shared bed, the two of them had discovered the
coveted secrets that Fern had been hankering after so
desperately.

She grinned now, languidly and sensually. The

urge to stretch like a contented cat was strong. Paul brought this out in her, this hunger, this eager anticipation that would initiate the intimate touching and kissing and moaning, the heated desire that would culminate in a feeling of intense satisfaction.

The secrets Paul had revealed had been startling and potent and utterly amazing. The enigma of what took place between a husband and wife would have been worth becoming mortal for, all by itself. But there was more to it than that. Paul was dedicated to her, devoted to her. As she was to him. They had each other in good times and in bad. In sickness and in health. And only death could separate them.

That kind of love was worth more than all the gold that was hoarded by the leprechauns in Sidhe.

It was then that she saw the first of the flickering lights outside the window. Tiny glowing bodies that darted and hovered just outside the glass. Fern laughed softly, ecstatic to have her friends come to visit.

"I'm happy," she told them. "Happier than I ever thought possible."

Paul reached around her, tucking his arms snugly underneath her breasts, his breath warm against her ear.

"I'm happy, too," he murmured.

She twisted around and saw that he wasn't talking to her. He was addressing the pixies who had come to call on them. Although Fern couldn't see their tiny faces, she could feel their joy. They were delighted that she was happy, and they were wishing her well.

Paul scooped her up into his arms and kissed her soundly on the mouth. Desire sparked, then raged deep in her belly, and she was eager to please and be pleased by him.

"I need you," he whispered. "Let's go to bed."

"By me heart," she swore the oath softly, "I believe that's the best idea I've heard all day."

*   *   *   *   *

If you enjoyed what you just read,
then we've got an offer you can't resist!

Take 2 bestselling
love stories FREE!
Plus get a FREE surprise gift!

Clip this page and mail it to Silhouette Reader Service

IN U.S.A.	IN CANADA
3010 Walden Ave.	P.O. Box 609
P.O. Box 1867	Fort Erie, Ontario
Buffalo, N.Y. 14240-1867	L2A 5X3

YES! Please send me 2 free Silhouette Romance® novels and my free surprise gift. After receiving them, if I don't wish to receive anymore, I can return the shipping statement marked cancel. If I don't cancel, I will receive 6 brand-new novels every month, before they're available in stores! In the U.S.A., bill me at the bargain price of $21.34 per shipment plus 25¢ shipping and handling per book and applicable sales tax, if any*. In Canada, bill me at the bargain price of $24.68 plus 25¢ shipping and handling per book and applicable taxes**. That's the complete price and a savings of at least 10% off the cover prices—what a great deal! I understand that accepting the 2 free books and gift places me under no obligation ever to buy any books. I can always return a shipment and cancel at any time. Even if I never buy another book from Silhouette, the 2 free books and gift are mine to keep forever.

209 SDN DU9H
309 SDN DU9J

Name	(PLEASE PRINT)	
Address	Apt.#	
City	State/Prov.	Zip/Postal Code

* Terms and prices subject to change without notice. Sales tax applicable in N.Y.
** Canadian residents will be charged applicable provincial taxes and GST.
  All orders subject to approval. Offer limited to one per household and not valid to current Silhouette Romance® subscribers.
  ® are registered trademarks of Harlequin Books S.A., used under license.

SROM03   ©1998 Harlequin Enterprises Limited

COMING NEXT MONTH

#1726 HER SECOND-CHANCE MAN—Cara Colter

High school outsider Jessica Moran could never forget golden boy Brian Kemp's teasing smile—or the unlikely friendship they'd shared when she'd helped him heal a sick dog. So when Brian walked back into her life fourteen years later, with another sick puppy and a rebellious teenager in tow, Jessica knew she was being given a second chance at love....

#1727 CINDERELLA'S SWEET-TALKING MARINE—Cathie Linz

Men of Honor

Captain Ben Kozlowski was a marine with a mission! Sworn to protect the sister of a fallen soldier, he marched into Ellie Jensen's life and started issuing orders. But this sassy single mother had some rules of her own, and before long, Ben found himself wanting to promise to love and honor more than to serve and protect.

#1728 CALLIE'S COWBOY—Madeline Baker

When Native American rancher Cade Kills Thunder came to her rescue on a remote Montana highway, Callie Walker was in heaven. The man was even more handsome than the male models that graced the covers of her romance novels! Would Callie be able to capture this rugged rancher's attention...and his heart?

#1729 THE BOSS'S BABY SURPRISE—Lilian Darcy

Soulmates

Cecilia Rankin kept having the weirdest dreams, like visions of her sexy boss, Nick Delaney, soothing a crying child. But when her dream began to come true and Nick ended up guardian of his sister's baby, Celie knew that Nick really *was* the man of her dreams.

SRCNM0604